NIGHTSHIFT

Victoria Hancox

NIGHTSHIFT

The Cluster of Echoes: Book 1

2nd Edition Published 2021

www.victoriahancox.com

ISBN: 9781089485285

Also in The Cluster of Echoes series:

The Alchemist's Folly (Book 2)

The Phantom Self (Book 3)

The Misanthrope – A Novella

INTRODUCTION

NIGHTSHIFT is an interactive story with a difference. You don't have to choose your character's attributes. You're just a normal human doing a normal job who finds themselves in a strange and dangerous place.

Oh, did I not mention the danger? Yes, you're being hunted and if they catch you… well, let's just say, there are many ways to skin a cat and many ways to die.

There's no dice to throw and let's face it — if there were, you'd only cheat. Oh no, you won't get through by winning battles, being lucky and you definitely have no spells, potions or swords.

What will get you through to the end of the nightshift is the knowledge and skills you already have but remember to record all the evidence and hints you find, too! You'll find space for this at the back of the book. And if you're feeling a bit lost, you can download the floorplans from
https://www.victoriahancox.com/nightshift

You just might make it out if you can piece together the clues and figure out the puzzles.

If you're ready, we can start. Turn to section **1**.

1

You wake up with a start and the darkness confuses you at first. Where are you? With your heart thudding in your chest, you grope aimlessly around, trying to get your bearings. You're lying across functional and slightly sticky faux-leather chairs. Oh, that's right. You give a relieved sigh as your eyes adjust to the gloominess and you can now make out the furniture in the small break room. How long had you been asleep?

It had been an intense nightshift in the operating department so far. You hurtled straight into an emergency aortic aneurysm, who, despite everyone's best efforts, died on the table. And once you'd cleaned that up, the phone rang, warning you that an urgent neuro case was on its way. At least, that'd gone better — clot removed and patient patched up, but it was hard to say just how much brain damage was already done. That was 3:30.

You and Nancy had trudged off the break rooms, where Nancy settled down with a Netflix programme and you'd gone off to catch some much-needed sleep. You always suffered from insomnia when you were working the nightshift.

You gradually notice the silence. Maybe Nancy fell asleep too. But there's something else… And, for that matter, what woke you up? You stand up, cracking your spine as you stretch, then go to the door. As soon as you open it though, it is clear that something is definitely wrong. The corridor is dark. Who's turned the lights off? The lights are never turned off. And then you hear it: a lazy, heavy drip-drip. You think about calling out to Nancy but your throat is constricted, so you inch towards the entrance of the other break room, fingertips walking over the wall. You draw closer and closer and can now see a flickering light in the darkness. There's no sound but the television illuminates the scene.

You gasp. An involuntary intake of shock and your hand automatically covers your mouth. You stare — you can't stop staring — and you know that Nancy is beyond help. She is slumped over on her side, throat slashed from ear to ear, and stab wounds all over her body. An ever-widening pool of blood is collecting on the floor as it oozes down from her neck in slowly coagulating drops.

At that moment, you notice them. The footprints. The bloodied footprints walking away from the corpse and into the corridor. It breaks your paralysis and you moan. He's still here. The murderer's still here. For a second, you feel an overwhelming urge to slump on the floor and wait till he finds you. But then, no. You don't want to die. You have to get out.

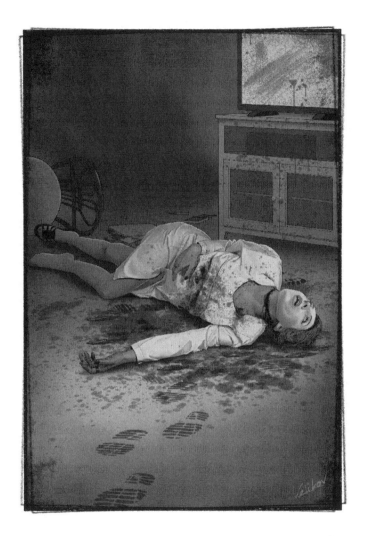

You think quickly now. The Intensive Care Unit. Plenty of people there. Plenty of help. That's the best place. You pad almost silently down the small corridor, pause at the end, then decisively open the door and slip into the main part of the operating department. You freeze, holding your breath. Listening. The door closes behind you with a gentle whoosh. It's a giveaway. If he's heard that, he knows exactly where you are. You stand there like a statue for an eternity, although it's probably only seconds, then set off again, running steadily towards the locked door at the far end. The door that connects the theatres to ICU. Only a few more steps, just a few more steps. You slide into the alcove, trying to breathe without making a sound. You feel sick, but you're nearly there. All you have to do now is put in the code to unlock the door.

And that's when you hear it. A distinct cough followed by a door opening and the footsteps of someone heavy. Someone confident. And... someone heading this way.

Your brain explodes in a blaze of panic, all neurones firing at once. Get out! You turn to the keypad, remembering only that the code is the first 4 prime numbers. He's getting closer. You can hear his breath. You can smell him. You've only got one chance.

With your sweating, slippery fingers, what number do you type in?

2357	Turn to **230**
1235	Turn to **97**
1357	Turn to **351**

2

You are padding softly down the corridor, deep in thought, when a screech cuts through the stillness. You gasp and spin around but there's nothing in the passageway. The noise came from your left, so maybe a stray and wounded animal has got into the neuro-surgical unit there. If you want to enter the unit to investigate, turn to **268**. However, on your right, is the prayer room. You've never been in there before, but if you want to see it now, turn to **11**. Or you could simply carry on along the passageway (turn to **113**).

3

You need to finish your spell before the demon comes up with something new. You pick up your concoction from the counter and prepare to add the final ingredient — the dying breath. If you know how to do this, you should have received the code words. Turn the words into a number using: A=1, B=2, C=3 ….. Z=26. **Add** *this* number to the current section, then turn to the section with that new, bigger number. If you don't know the words, you cannot finish the spell but rest assured — Jezebeth has plenty of tricks up her sleeve to get the better of you. Your nightshift ends here.

4

You speak the words aloud: *An atrium or an infection, Gain access through the fourth section.* A soft click disturbs the silence and when you try the handle, the door swings open. You step into a golden room. It's a rich shade that manages to be both opulent and tacky and is lit only by a multitude of candles. On the wall opposite is an oil painting of a woman wearing a white lab coat. The only furniture in the room is a table with a dissecting dish on it but it isn't empty! You edge closer and recognise the organ lying in it — a uterus. The door closes behind you and when you turn to check whether you're locked in, you see a heart nailed to it. The number '6' is scrawled in blood underneath. Just as you're wondering how many more body parts does Jezebeth have in her secret room, a voice beckons you. You look around and see the woman in the portrait adjust her glasses and peer myopically at you.

'Yes, you. Come here. We don't have all day, you know.' You go over to the painting, completely at a loss about what to ask it. Luckily, the woman doesn't have time for your hesitancy, and she continues in a rapid monologue with a New England accent. 'Number 6 was Elizabeth. An intimidating witch with impressive powers of crafting spells. It's a dangerous ability that Jezebeth craved but also feared. That's why she keeps it trapped in here, but if you plan to concoct your own mixture to destroy the demon, this is where you need to do it. You must be prepared before you face her. Now I can't help you much more, but first you must choose the vessel in which you will blend the ingredients.' With that, the portrait becomes silent and still again. You look through your bag at all the items you've gathered so far.

Which item do you pick to craft your own spell in?

A wooden bowl	Turn to **150**
A golden goblet	Turn to **379**
A silver chalice	Turn to **229**

5

She looks at you with confusion and slight annoyance.

'How am I supposed to know that? I've just told you, I'm not a witch. It's been over 400 years and people *still* think I'm a witch!' With that, she gives a little stamp of her foot and walks out of the door. You've had enough of the damp stench in this room, so you decide to hobble out too. Turn to **368**.

6

You open the door, dreading what lies beyond. During your training, you spent a day with a pathologist and that experience was enough to last a lifetime. It's not as bad as you expected though. There is a body on the post-mortem table, but it's shrouded by a white sheet and otherwise, the mortuary looks as clean and sterile as your operating theatres. To the left is the floor-to-ceiling bank of individual fridges for the corpses, numbered 1 to 24 and to your right, the washing and storage areas. You think this is the right place to find the exit but if that's all you know, you're never going to get out. However, if someone told you a clue, maybe you'll get lucky…

What should you do?

Open fridge 1	Turn to **141**
Open fridge 12	Turn to **63**
Open fridge 23	Turn to **225**
Open fridge 24	Turn to **327**

7

At the end of the ivy tunnel there is a door with five-petalled, blue flowers painted on it. You brush away some strands of ivy to reveal a sign: Welcome to Periwinkle Ward — Paediatrics. You try to open the door, but it doesn't budge. Locked? You're about to retrace your steps back when the foliage shifts to reveal a large iron key in the lock. Maybe that's just heightened security for the Children's Ward, you think. You turn the key and step through into a warm, blush-pink painted corridor. The ward is silent other than a persistent draught whistling in, but then you hear footsteps in the distance. It sounds like someone is approaching the ward from the opposite side. If you want to stand your ground and see who this is, turn to **346**, but if you think it'd be wiser to hide, turn to **161**.

8

You walk swiftly towards the exit of the operating department and unlock the doors, but when you step out into the main thoroughfare, your heart sinks. You were hoping it would look normal; that you'd finally woken up from a nightmare but no. If anything, it looks even worse. Ceiling tiles are hanging down from the twisted metal struts and there are deep, long gouges in the few vestiges of plaster on the walls. If you didn't know better, you'd say that they were claw marks, but it couldn't be, could it? You take a deep breath and try to plan what to do now. You can either go left (turn to **106**) or right (turn to **166**).

9

Back at the junction, you can either decide to turn left and head to the ward exit (turn to **50**) or you could investigate the room where you heard the children's voices if you haven't done so already (turn to **182**).

10

Success! You step back onto the Persian rug in the foyer and thanks to your shaking legs, collapse onto the floor. The skin over your spine is still stinging, but once you've calmed down, you place the box in front of you and open the lid. Nestled in purple velvet, is a black-handled, double-bladed knife — the inscription on the inside of the lid declares this to be the **Athame knife**. You place it carefully in your bag and stand up.

What now? Look at the statue (turn to **244**) or head for the double doors (turn to **41**)?

You step in, let the door gently close behind you and stand there agog. It's a small room with no windows and it's brown. The carpet, the walls, the ceiling are all a deep, rich brown. It's like standing in a vat of warm chocolate. Or a grave, your inner voice unhelpfully chips in with. There are a few cheap wooden chairs with brown velvet upholstery that have seen better days and at the far end, a full-length stained-glass mural. It depicts a forest with lush green leaves on the trees and a deer, a badger and a crow lurking in the undergrowth. Whilst it makes sense to have a nature scene as the focal point instead of religious images, this seems gloomy, disturbing even. You're not sure what it is but there's something distinctly creepy about it, and you feel a sudden urge to destroy it. Although breaking glass when there's a killer stalking the hospital isn't the most sensible thing to do, if you want to follow your instincts and smash the mural, you should turn to **48**. If you'd prefer to stay quiet and leave the prayer room, you could head across the corridor to the neuro-surgical ward if you haven't done so already (turn to **268**) or just continue along the passageway.— go left (turn to **338**) or go right (turn to **113**).

12

The pool is like an antiquated Victorian spa but it's clean, peaceful and the water does look inviting. You edge closer and suddenly hear a laugh. You spin round and see a green-skinned woman stood behind you. She smiles an unpleasant grin with tiny, shark-like teeth.

'Who are you?' you ask but she doesn't answer. She just smiles, then abruptly feints forward. You shift backwards and lose your balance. For a second, you teeter, then gravity takes you and you fall into the water with a splash. The green-skinned woman laughs again. You flap around, then realise that you're in the shallow end and stand up.

'Ha ha. Very funny,' you say and start wading towards the pool edge. Just as you grab the side and prepare to heave yourself up, she puts her hand on the top of your head and pushes down. She has more force than you'd have thought possible. Your feet slip out from underneath and you plunge under the surface. You rise back up but instead of emerging from the water, you smash into a barrier. It's like the pool's surface has frozen over. Instantly overwhelmed by panic, you hit out, trying to break through, but you can't. Already your lungs are on fire. You have to breathe, but you can't breathe. You can see her crouched at the side, simply watching you with a detached curiosity. You plead with your eyes, but she just smiles. Finally, you take in a huge breath of water and feel absolute agony as it burns your lungs. But it doesn't last long. The darkness quickly closes in.

The green-skinned woman watches your body bobbing about in the water, then grows bored and walks away.

13

As the lid comes off, you're expecting the strong smell of formaldehyde but there's nothing. You give a brief shrug of the shoulders then insert your hand in. Your fingers close around the tongue but it's a slippery organ and you can't quite grab it. You're so focused on the task that you don't realise the jar is getting smaller and smaller, until you finally try to withdraw and find that your hand is stuck tight. Trying not to panic, you pull at the glass, almost dislocating your thumb, but your hand won't shift. You have no option but to smash the jar against the edge of the bench. Turn to **33**.

14

There is a long pause, then finally the demon slumps back on her tail and shakes her head at you.

'Do you have any idea what you've just done?' You look down at the fractured amulet with crumbs of lapis lazuli strewn around and shake your head.

'You may have won a battle. After all, I can't kill you or take you over now. But you haven't won the war. You've trapped us here, in this realm, together, for all eternity.' You open your mouth to protest but one look at Jezebeth's face tells you she's not joking or, for once, not lying. You're never going home now.

15

You give the keys an impatient jiggle but either they're old and rusty, or you chose the wrong order. Erichtho spits in disgust at you and gobs of bloodied saliva spray across your face. You presume that means it was the wrong order. You begin pleading to try again but the crone has already scrambled to her feet, taking the chest with her. She crouches back down over the corpse and resumes her meal. You blew it. You have no option but to leave the room. Turn to **227**.

16

You have to stand on tiptoes in order to reach down into the bowels of this machine. Sweat is trickling over your forehead and stinging your eyes. When you finally get a fingertip on the mysterious object, it swivels around, out of reach again. You give a final desperate lunge and… Got it! With ragged breaths, you pull the object out and see that it's a fancy-looking, white-handled knife. On closer inspection, it has a green substance smeared along the blade, which seems to be… With an ear drum bursting shriek, the machine starts up, blades whirring, and the rag doll is pushing your arm back in. Deeper and deeper. You fight and yell, but it's just too strong. And then, you feel a pain like you couldn't ever imagine, as the blades macerate your fingers, hand and arm into a pulp. All you can hear now is a heavy, repetitive thud, thud, thud. Are you dying? Turn to **271**.

17

As you approach the junction in the x-ray department, you see the figure in blue scrubs again. It darts out from a nearby door and runs quickly up the corridor towards the children's ward. You shout out and rush forward but by the time you get there, the figure has gone. You stand there frustrated with your hands on your hips and in the window of the exit doors ahead, you catch a glimpse of your reflection — standing there, hands on hips, in blue scrubs! You gasp. It can't be! You try to recall the figure's face, but it was hidden. If you want to track down the figure, take this passageway and head towards the children's ward (turn to **115**). If you'd rather continue straight ahead and back down the corridor, turn to **354**.

18

With your answer, it gives a satisfied nod and says decisively, 'The Crow knows about the exit; you will have to ask the Crow.'

'Where do I find the Crow?' you ask, although you can't quite believe you're having this conversation. But as suspected, it simply smiles and shakes its head. Damn. Only one question allowed. But then it waves its wrinkled and calloused hand over the desk counter and, as if a finger is wiping through the dirt, the following words appear: ROAM OR PYRE. You look quizzically at it, one eyebrow raised.

'The choice faced by all witches,' it sighs. 'That's your clue to find the Crow.'

'Clue? Like a crossword puzzle? Or an anagram?' With this last suggestion, it lowers its head once more but says nothing. You look down at the letters ROAMORPYRE and have an inkling of an idea. When you next look up, the person has gone and you're alone again. If you haven't done so already and you want to explore the cafeteria, turn to **180**. If you'd rather head now to the swampy corridor, turn to **70**.

19

Once you've asked your question, the Crow regards you with flinty eyes. Slowly, it deliberately shakes its head from side to side.

'I had high hopes for you, but you choose to waste your opportunities, because you simply can't focus. Well, you get all you deserve.' And with that, it struts off. You try to follow but your hands and legs won't move. They're too heavy. You can't even move your eyes now and you have no choice but to stare fixedly at the mural.

Just before it all goes black forever, you see a stained-glass version of yourself appear, peering out from behind an oak tree, trapped in the glass mural forever.

20

You look tentatively at the bottles — laudanum, elixir of opium and tincture of morphine — and are considering taking a sniff, when a thought occurs to you. Could Jezebeth's secret room be close by? If you know how to search for it, you should do that now. If not, you decide that it's probably not a good idea to sniff potent narcotics and go to search either the hallucinogens (turn to **118**) or the sleeping potions (turn to **263**).

21

For a second, you panic, thinking that you've lost the tiny key, but it's just tucked into the folds of the bag. The clasp unlocks with a 'ping', and you open the lid.

The book must be either very valuable or very important to have been locked up in this box and it looks it. The cover is a dark burgundy embossed leather with the intricate wording: Book of Shadows. You can feel a strange vibration in your hands; a thrumming that seems to be coming from the book itself. Is this tome resisting you? Well, let's see, you think, and you open the cover to see what the contents are. Turn to **196**.

Despite the dark blue hue of the walls, the brightness of the operating lights exposes everything in stark detail. Especially the corpse lying on the table. A young woman with her long, dark hair hanging over the side and dull, glazed eyes staring beyond you. Oh, and a huge gaping incision in her abdomen. Did something happen that interrupted the surgery, so they had to leave her here? You creep closer and your expert eyes take in the stomach and intestines but... hang on. Where's her liver? This looks less like the sort of surgery you know and more like a harvesting. Suddenly, the operating light starts shifting, moving steadily from the dead woman to the other side of the room. Eventually it stops, the beam of light aimed directly at the operations register and you wonder if any details of this so-called surgery were recorded. If you want to examine the register, turn to **37**. If you think that it may be more prudent to find a weapon here, turn to **246**.

You approach the doorway and see an eerie green light emanating from within. It's an office and the computer monitor has its green standby light on. You gasp. Electricity? Internet? However, when you rush to the desk, you quickly realise that, not only is there no actual computer, but the monitor is not even plugged in. You can't bring yourself to ask how it's lit up if it has no power. As you stand up to leave, you notice the cursor flashing on the screen, then suddenly a stream of letters appears. It says:

'When I'm small, I'm the longest and when I'm large, I'm the shortest. What part of the body am I?'

Seriously? A riddle? You shake your head, disbelievingly.

However, if you find yourself in a location which might be connected to the riddle's *answer*, **add 50** to the section number you find yourself at, then turn to that section.

There's nothing else here in this office, so you head back towards the exit, but before you leave, a notice board on the wall catches your eye. You're not sure why but you feel drawn to two items pinned up there — the off-duty roster and a postcard. If you wish to examine the roster, turn to **292**. If you'd prefer to study the postcard, turn to **179**. If you'd rather ignore this strange compulsion and leave the unit, turn to **311**.

24

You cup your hands into the water, then lean over to rinse your face, when something makes you open your eyes. You scream and cast the cupped water away. The pool is swarming with millions of tiny, wriggling centipedes. You wipe your hands desperately against your legs and back away. You were about to rub all those centipedes against your skin; into your eyes… You gag at the thought. On shaky legs, you leave the room and head for the exit (turn to **171**).

25

It's a relief to be in this passageway. It's wide and airy with skylights in the vaulted roof and the bright sunshine warms your bones after the gloom of the asylum. As you approach the geriatric ward, you see another corridor shooting off to the right. There are no signs, so you're not sure where it leads to, but if you want to investigate, turn to **333**. However, if you'd prefer to go straight on to the ward (turn to **355**).

26

Charpentier heads straight on without hesitation. You watch him go, then shout, 'What about going right?'
The cat's fur bristles up and he gives a sharp shake.

'No, no, no. That's a very bad idea. Jinny the Witch lives down there. You'd never make it out alive. If you go there, you're by yourself.'
Turn back to **126** and decide where to go.

27

It's quite a sight and for a few seconds, you simply stare at this medieval figure, until finally it speaks.

'What do you want? I'm busy,' it barks at you, the voice muffled by the beak.

'I want to get out of here,' you eventually stutter. It sighs impatiently, then says, 'Well?' Its left hand is outstretched waiting for you to put something in it.

'I haven't got all day!'

You have to quickly decide which item to give him. Do you hand over the obsidian amulet (turn to **57**), the dried bluebell (turn to **282**) or the crushed sea eagle talons (turn to **169**)?

28

As you inch closer towards the voice, you realise that the refrigerators are packed with blood transfusion bags. This is the blood bank! Just as you're taking this in, you sense a movement and see the woman. She is sat on a plain wooden chair with only one leg. The woman, that is, not the chair!

'My name is Empusa,' she states, delicately wiping a smear of blood from her lips. You cannot hide the look of disdain that crosses your face — she was *drinking* the blood — so Empusa retorts, 'Well, you'd consider me a monster if I were to just sup it directly from the neck.' You have no answer to that and after a few seconds of silence, the one-legged woman asks, 'I know a lot about this place and what's happening. What would you like to know?'

If you would like to ask how Jezebeth captured Carmichael, turn to **393** but if you'd prefer to know whether you are a witch with a power, turn to **129**.

You sit down on the grass next to her and she takes your hands in hers. She smiles gently, as she studies your palms. You panic, thinking she wants to chop your hands off like Carmichael did, but before you can jump up, she lets go, leans back and looks at you. In a soft voice, she says, 'I'm pleased to see that you're intact. You have done well to survive so far. I have hope for you, although your battle is not over yet. Did my dogs scare you? They always get so excited whenever I arrive.'

'Who are you?' You surreptitiously check her out but as far as you can see, there seems to be no body parts missing.

'I am Hecate. You are wearing my ring. I look after my babies.'

The sudden change of subject confuses you, but then you realise that she means the gravestones. Now you understand. This is where the newborn and stillborn babies were buried. Hecate looks fondly over the small cemetery and continues, 'The yew tree was planted in graveyards because they thought that the roots grew through the skeletons of the dead and kept them from roaming the Earth.'

Well, that was an image that you didn't need to have in your head! Was this all she could offer you? Visions of nightmares! But Hecate hasn't noticed your discomfort and is still talking.

'Jezebeth will not let you go so easily — she will try once more to confound you, but I will give you this.' She hands you a small piece of folded paper and as you start to open it, she gasps and clutches your hand.

'What you hold there is a powder. Aconite. Otherwise known as Carmichael's Monkshood.' She smirks and you get the feeling that, as gentle as she seems, you really wouldn't want to cross her.

'Is it poison?' you ask, placing the paper packet carefully into your pocket. Hecate nods.

'Yes, but only on the mannequins she sends. Beware false friends. This has no effect on a demon.' With that, she closes her eyes, leans back and melts into the tree. Her outstretched legs become the protruding roots, her face, the knots in the bark.

You go back inside now, heading further along the corridor (turn to **301**).

30

You are standing back in the corridor going over what you've just seen, when you realise with mounting horror that the black, wispy cocoon has vanished. You look left and right but there's no sign of it. And then the thought occurs to you and with utter dread, you look up.

You let out a whoosh of air and a softly muttered curse. It's not above you either, although there are black streaks along the ceiling, tracing its path away to who knows where. Still, you have to decide where _you_ should go now — you can't wait around here. You could continue along the passageway by going right (turn to **159**) or left (turn to **299**). Alternatively, you could investigate the general ward opposite if you haven't done so already (turn to **45**).

31

You reach out, grasping blindly for the door handle. You don't know anymore where you are or even who you are! You hear a noise from behind, but all you can focus on is getting out. Somehow you know that this fog will lift if you can just get out! Finally, you pull open the door, but before you can take another step, there is a streak of movement, then a sharp pain in your wrist. You cry out and clutch the bleeding hand to your chest, watching as a small brown snake slithers off under the gurney. The child has gone. You stumble out of the room and lean against the wall. When you eventually pluck up the courage to examine the wound, you're surprised to see two small scabs where the fangs punctured you. No swelling or redness, and no blood. It looks almost healed. You can't imagine that's a good thing, but there's nothing you can do about it now. You can either head right and go back to the junction (turn to **9**) or head left and leave the ward (turn to **62**).

32

The sheets tumble onto the floor in a tangled, blood-stained heap. The writhing becomes more frantic and you take a step back. Is it a rat? You see a small leg emerge from underneath the linen. *A baby?* But wait... Something doesn't look right. It doesn't look like skin or flesh; it looks like wood. And now you can see the smooth joints and the strings. As it is finally revealed, you realise with a sinking heart that it is a marionette. A puppet. Its carved face is angry, with a long protruding nose and rose-painted lips. It is also covered in blood, almost like it's just been born, then thrown away…

You slam the door, leaving the Delivery Room and that abomination as fast as you can and head further along the corridor (turn to **119**).

33

The jar smashes, splintering into thousands of pieces onto the floor and making the mist ripple away. The preservative fluid splashes your scrubs and as you jump back, you catch a glimpse of the tongue lying motionless like a lump of meat before the mist returns and closes over it, then nothing. You wait but still nothing. Finally, you decide that this is a waste of time and you should leave. You turn to head for the door.

Stood directly behind you is a woman. You scream, jump away from her but skid in the fluid. You fall, feeling tiny shards pierce your skin. The woman looks surprised then smiles.

'I have little time but thank you from the bottom of my heart. Tongues are how we communicate and mine has the power to talk to animals. You have freed me and now this power is yours. Whenever you need to use the power, speak the word: GLOSSAL.'

'Wait!' you cry, 'What does this murderer want from me? I have no powers.'

'All women have the power to create and nurture life. Men don't. Robert Carmichael envied this and thanks to his mother, hated women — it was a dangerous combination. Many fell under his knife as he tried to understand the power. At first, he was shunned from his profession, then eventually hunted for his crimes. He disappeared without a trace in 1898, but, of course, he didn't disappear. Somehow, he had learnt about the real powers of witches and he made this world. He's continued his deadly search ever since and grows stronger with each power. Maybe you do have a power, maybe you don't. It doesn't matter. He will rip you apart anyway, looking for it.'

As her words fade away, so does she. Her pale skin becoming transparent, while her white mane of hair falls and merges with the mist. Well, at least you have some answers, although not quite what you were hoping for. You've had enough of this place now, so you head for the exit. Turn to **233**.

34

The door opens to a narrow corridor with no windows, so you're relying on your pen torch. You hope its batteries will last... But you don't need a torch to realise that there's no swamp here. The smell has gone and there's no splashing sound as you walk, although your feet are still soaked and green with algae. You're not going to waste time trying to make sense of that though. You go past offices and small labs, but the doors are locked. Still, you feel compelled only by the large room at the end. *That's* where you want to go. But that door is locked too. You push your face up against the frosted glass, trying to peer through but no luck, although you're sure you can see something with a pink glow in there. After considering then dismissing a notion of breaking in, you head back out into the thoroughfare and continue heading towards the hospital entrance. Turn to **256**.

35

You carry on along the cold, empty passageway and when you take the right turn, see that it ends at a doorway and the door is ajar. If you want to see what lies beyond that door, turn to **257**, but if you've changed your mind and want to head back to the junction, turn to **197**.

36

You push open the door and walk into the apothecary. Along three of the four walls are oaken shelves filled with brown glass bottles of tinctures and below, hundreds of tiny wooden drawers concealing all manner of powders. In the middle of the room is a counter with delicate balancing scales and mortars. You knew from the sign of the serpent encircling the chalice that this was the pharmacy but it's none like you've ever known. You should explore this place, but which drugs will you inspect first?

Sleeping potions and ethers   Turn to **263**
Opium and pain killers   Turn to **20**
Hallucinogens   Turn to **118**

37

Instead of a patient's name, it just says '8'. The part where the surgery is described is totally blank and the surgeon's name is Lister. Well, that was useful, you think sarcastically. But maybe it was. Who knows? You've had enough of this abattoir though, so you head over to the scrub up area where the exit door is. Turn to **306**.

38

You have to lean in to reach the back of the furnace and suddenly, you have visions of the Witch in Hansel and Gretel trying to bundle you into an oven. You concentrate on rummaging around in the fine ash as a way to keep a lid on your rising hysteria, and your perseverance is rewarded when your fingers clip something solid; something metallic. Your first thought is: Great! An artificial hip! But you quickly realise that it's something more refined, especially when it gives a delicate tinkle. You extract yourself from the furnace and look at your prize. A **pewter hand bell**. You give a nod of satisfaction and put it in one of your pockets. You're thinking of checking out the other furnace when a noise from behind startles you. Turn to **121**.

39

Although you're not normally a violent person, you feel a burst of anger and determination to end this. You didn't ask for any of this and you're not going to end up with parts of you hacked off! Through a red mist, your hands grip her sinewy throat and a fierce rage tightens your fingers. She gazes at you with bulging but calm eyes, her toothless, stinking mouth gaping open. She doesn't resist or fight, but you still don't stop. You *can't* stop. Eventually, you realise that you can't hold this dead weight up anymore, so you let go, finally shocked by what has just happened. Her bony body crumples to the floor. You mutter, 'I had to do it' over and over again, but there's a distinct lack of conviction. You stagger backwards on weak legs until you're back in the corridor. Only then can you drag your eyes off the crone you've just killed and close the door. You slump to the floor, flipping between blaming this Hellish place for putting you in this intolerable position and self-loathing at what you've become. After some time, you wipe your eyes and get up. What's done is done. You need to keep moving. Turn to **227**.

40

You're not sure how it works but you pluck the Scarlet Pimpernel from behind your ear and with a flourish, ask:

'Who is telling the truth?'

The red petals start to fall off, which doesn't look promising, but when they reach the floor, a vortex pulls them round and round until there is a scarlet twister between you and the children. With a flurry, it whirls towards one of them, then collapses, cascading the petals like rain. They both giggle and the child underneath the petals says, 'That's right! I always tell the truth — it *is* the banishing colour!' The other child nods happily in agreement, then they continue the bridge-building game. If you still have The Book of Shadows, you could go to the chapter entitled 'The Powers of Colour' and remind yourself which colour is associated with 'banishing', but otherwise, there is nothing else to be gained from staying here, so you get up and leave (turn to **398**).

41

You push open the double doors and stride through, despite not knowing where you're heading. Down a short oak-panelled passageway, you emerge into a large chamber with a semi-circle of tiered seating. Is it a lecture theatre? No, wait. Instead of a podium for the lecturer, there's an operating table. Suddenly, it's clear. This is a Victorian operating theatre with its spectators' gallery. You gently touch the table, imagining the abject fear and pain suffered by the countless people held down and hacked at. Just as the thought crystallises in your mind — a Victorian surgeon — you hear a footstep behind you. If you possess the Athame knife, turn to **101**. If not, turn to **254**.

42

It's almost a relief when your feet sink back into the green mud. There was something about that place that just didn't feel right. You're about to squelch back down the corridor when a portrait catches your eye. You head curiously over to it and study the traditional oil painting of serious looking, Victorian men. Doctors, you presume. You read the accompanying notice and one name stands out: Dr Robert Carmichael. You look back at the man, third from the left. He's stocky with thick, dark sideburns and moustache and his expression is a scowl. You look at the painting a little longer then carry on down the corridor until you go past the shop again. There's no sign of anyone there now and you decide to keep going. At the end of the corridor, it takes a sharp left towards the A&E department and if you want to head there, turn to **146**. If you haven't done so already and you'd like to take a right into the hospital entrance foyer, turn to **343**.

43

You turn what you think is 180° and stagger forward with arms outstretched, but your desperate fingers clutch nothing but cold air. Hysteria is nearing a breaking point when finally, you touch something solid. Something flat and vertical. Please be the door, you implore. You have never been more relieved when you eventually find the handle and step back into the bright x-ray department. Turn to **189**.

44

You turn the corner and step out onto the grass. The scent of jasmine in the fresh air is beguiling, but the storm must be getting closer — dark, bruised clouds now fill the sky and the dogs have fallen silent. Is that a good sign…?

Despite your misgivings, it is a beautiful place, but then you notice the gravestones. A cluster of them underneath an old and gnarly yew tree. You venture forward and see the worn, lichen-covered words and dates. Some were only a day old; some never even breathed but they were all here, as if someone were caring for them. You gaze around then notice one stone away from the rest. After brushing the moss away, you read:

'Who lies here, nobody knows. No-one cries except the Crows. Beware of lies within the rose.' A shiver goes through you and you stand up.

You've had enough of this place, so you leave the garden and go back into the corridor (turn to **301**).

45

The door opens with only the faintest wheeze, but slams shut with a crash. Instantly there is an exodus — a mass of sharp claws skittering across the floor — and you picture a flood of rats streaming away. At least they're not streaming in *your* direction, but now you're dreading finding out why they were here in the first place. After all, vermin usually only go where there's easy access to food and in this place, that can only mean one thing. As you walk through the deserted ward, you look at each bed but there's no corpses. Nothing and yet you can smell something really bad. What is it? And where is it? Suddenly, you realise that you're looking too low. Arranged decoratively around the curtain rails surrounding one of the beds, like a Christmas garland, is a complete set of intestines. The purple coils swell then contract in a hypnotic wave and out of one torn end, comes an occasional drip of putrid thick liquid. You stare mesmerised for a while — does this *mean* anything? — then shake yourself out of it. You notice that the gut is draped around **bed number 5** but otherwise, you don't think there's anything else here. You leave the ward and head back out into the thoroughfare. Turn to **362**.

46

At first, you can't believe what you're seeing. It's the adjacent Renal Unit and it looks normal! You pull back, ready to yell through the small hole, but at the last second, see something and you pause, squinting again. It looks normal, doesn't it? Nurses walking back and forth, patients in beds, clean, no murders — just what you'd expect — but there it is again. A slight shimmer in the atmosphere. It's as if what you're seeing isn't really what you're seeing, as if two images are superimposed over each other. But that doesn't make sense, does it? And then it starts — a loud humming noise, the buzz of millions of insects. It fills your brain and finally, you step back from the notice board. Like a switch going off, the droning stops and all you can hear is the gurgling sound still coming from the second bay. You wish you knew what was going on, but something tells you that you're not going to find any answers here. You head for the exit. Turn to **162**.

47

Charpentier raises lazy eyelids at you, flips onto his back to give a huge, spine-breaking stretch, then effortlessly jumps onto his paws and pads across to you.

'Go left first to the x-ray department, but after that come back the same way and go down there.' He has no fingers to point with but gestures with a flick of his ear down the right-hand corridor.

'Why?' you ask, 'What's there?' But the cat ignores you and starts strolling down the glass corridor.

'Where are you going?' But Charpentier merely leaps up onto the windowsill and slinks out through the narrowest of gaps. You didn't even know the window was open but, in a heartbeat, the cat is gone. There's nothing else to do but return to **147** and choose the direction to head in.

48

The chair lurches through the air towards the sturdy mural glass. You envisage the chair either bouncing straight off or breaking into wooden pieces, but there is a deafening sound of shattered glass as the entire floor to ceiling pane collapses into thousands of shards. After a stunned pause, when the glass remnants have all fallen, you face the door, fully expecting the man to come bursting in. But nothing happens. Now that the gloomy forest scene is no more, you feel lighter somehow. Make a note of the codeword **SHARDS** and leave the prayer room. You could now head over to the neuro-surgical ward if you haven't done so already (turn to **268**) or you could just carry on along the passageway — go left (turn to **338**) or go right (turn to **113**).

You get to your feet, wincing with every movement. Your entire body feels injured and each step now is agony, but you persevere on, hoping to get to the end of this black cave. It feels like an eternity but in reality, it's only five minutes later when your outstretched fingers touch the wooden surface of a door. You've reached the exit. Turn to **203**.

50

After a short distance, you reach the doors and leave the ward, stepping over the blue flowers which have been strewn there. Just ahead of you is a T-junction, but when you arrive there, you see that the right corridor is a thin, cold, concrete tunnel that seems to be sloping downwards and looks very unappealing. Looking left, you see that the passageway continues to a plain white door with the Bowl of Hygieia printed on it. You decide to head for this door (turn to **36**).

51

Trying to quash the rising sense of panic, you desperately think of how to summon Jezebeth. You call out her name. Nothing. You start pulling out drawers. Nothing. You empty your bag onto the floor, and just when you are rifling through the contents, searching for a clue, you hear the pharmacy door open. You look up, breathing rapidly and very, very scared. It is the assassin. Still dressed in black. Still carrying a knife and still obviously planning to kill you. He takes a step forward. If you earlier accidently inhaled furnace ash, turn to **390**. If you avoided breathing in the cremains, turn to **266**.

52

You inch silently into the Intensive Care Unit and soon reach the first bay, but to your intense disappointment, can see that it is clearly empty. The beds have rusted frames, some with torn mattresses, others with brown-stained sheets still on them, but no patients and no nurses. There are drip stands scattered over the floor and cobwebs drape from the curtain rails. At first, you can only hear your own heart thudding but then, you hear another noise. It's coming from the second bay. A gurgling, choking sound. A patient? You peer around the corner but can't make anything out, although you do notice an open door in the far wall. You're not sure what this room is but if you decide to head over to it, turn to **23**. On the other hand, if you think you should try to find the choking patient, turn to **186**.

53

You pull the door fully open, catching the mop as it slides to the floor. The room is small and dark and you can just make out some linen bags in the corner. They are crammed full of stained sheets. Suddenly, a movement catches your eye. It's one of the laundry bags. It looks as though something is wriggling around in there. If you want to find out what it is, turn to **316**. Alternatively, you could just leave this room and head further along the corridor (turn to **119**) or if you haven't done so already, you could pull back the curtains at the other side of the room (turn to **252**).

54

The jet-black smoke spirals up to the ceiling. Both you and Jezebeth watch it in stunned silence, but then you hear that mocking laughter again. The demon leers at you, licking a spindly tongue over one of its fangs and you realise that, although black is the correct colour, you must have made a wrong decision in an earlier part of the spell. You start to feel a strange sensation through your body, as Jezebeth begins to take control. The end can't be too far away but before that happens, you quickly think about all the items you've collected. Maybe one of these could be useful. Which amulet do you select?

The one made of Lapis lazuli   Turn to **384**
The one made of obsidian   Turn to **168**

55

There seems to be nothing else of interest here, so you look around, wondering what to do next. Out of the corner of your eye, you sense a movement, a flash of colours and when you look back, there's someone sat at the Information Desk. You gasp in shock, but the person merely smiles benignly with an incline of the head. Its thickened skin has white whiskers sprouting all over, and it has a crumpled, coarse, albeit human-like, appearance.

'How may I help you?' it asks, gesturing at the 'Information' sign, as if that explained anything.

You have a sudden worry that you have only one chance to ask a question, so you think rapidly: What's the best question to ask?

'How do I get out of here?' you eventually say. It regards you thoughtfully, then says, almost to itself, 'Mm, I remember that. Was it in the basement or the attic? It was one or the other, I'm sure.' It peters out, as it muses on the whereabouts of the exit, then squints fixedly at you. If you have recorded the word SHARDS, turn to **145**. If not, turn to **18**.

56

At the junction, you can either turn left, which will take you back past the glass corridor (turn to **391**) or go right to the rest of the x-ray department if you haven't been there already (turn to **204**).

57

The figure gives a frustrated shake of its head, its beak hitting the side of the door frame. It grabs the amulet from you and throws it far down the corridor. You turn to look where it lands and when you turn back, the door is already closing. You cry, 'No! Wait' but it's too late. You've lost your chance to find a way out and now it's only a matter of time before *he* catches you.

58

You push open the door and are almost blinded. For a second, you think it's just sunlight, but when your eyes finally adjust, you realise that the walls are painted a vivid yellow and you're not alone anymore. There is a young nurse sat in one of the chairs and opposite her are three elderly men. You approach the nurse but before you can ask her anything, she simply wags her finger at you.

'You may speak with one but only one of these fine gentlemen. Make your choice. There is Samael, Nathanael and Daniel.'

There's not much to tempt you with any of them. Samael seems to be concertedly rolling a small piece of excrement between his fingers; Nathanael is wearing urine-soaked pyjamas and Daniel has an impressively long string of drool hanging from his mouth. You consider your options.

Talk with Samael	Turn to **158**
Talk with Nathanael	Turn to **240**
Talk with Daniel	Turn to **356**
Leave the day room	Turn to **315**

The nearest thing is an empty glass. You snatch it up and raise your arm.

'What on Earth do you think you're doing?' a haughty voice asks. You freeze, arm still in the air, before yelling, 'What am I doing? What are *you* doing? That's disgusting!'

'Adjusting the position of an electrode is disgusting, is it? What? Because I'm using my mouth? I'm a cat! How am I supposed to move it? You idiot!'
You slowly lower your arm and glare at the feline, who, being a feline, glares right back at you. There is an awkward silence until you put the glass back onto the bedside locker and ask, 'Who are you? And who is *that*?'

'My name is Charpentier and that, as you so rudely put it, is my patient. I'm a chemist by profession but one could go absolutely insane in this place through boredom, so I decided to tinker with a bit of neurology. Fascinating stuff!'
You regard the cat for a few more seconds — could he be an ally or is this a ruse to trick you?

'Do you know anything about Carmichael or Jezebeth?' you ask. Charpentier rolls his eyes and gives a sharp flick of the tail.

'I do know that Jezebeth has a secret room in which certain objects are kept safe. Things that could do harm if they fall into the wrong hands. I don't know where it is though — hence it being a secret room, I suppose — although I do know a lot about this place. Cats can prowl around anywhere, you know. There are some advantages which make up for not having opposable thumbs. Are you planning to do harm to

Carmichael and Jezebeth?' Charpentier casually licks a paw while he waits for your answer. What do you say?

Yes, I'm going to kill them   Turn to **309**
No, I just want to go home   Turn to **96**

60

You walk away from the greenhouse and to the stairwell, then stand in front of the door with the pentacle painted on it. The 5-pointed star. No. 5. The intestines. You wonder for a second if the door is still locked but the bee kept her word and the door swings open easily and silently. You head down the stairs. And down. And down. Until finally, you reach the basement. A basement that you never knew even existed. You step out of the stairwell into a small foyer that's dimly lit by an ancient lightbulb, swinging from the low ceiling. There are two doors directly ahead of you — one is a storeroom, the other a toilet. A door on the left leads to the furnace room and the one on the right takes you to the mortuary. None of them sound particularly tempting, but you can't stay here, so which do you choose?

Storeroom   Turn to **164**
Toilet   Turn to **195**
Furnace   Turn to **219**
Mortuary   Turn to **6**

61

Further on, you see something attached halfway up the wall. That certainly doesn't look normal! You edge closer to find out what it is but all you can conclude is that it's a black wispy mass. It's only the size of a watermelon but it looks suspiciously like a cocoon and you're sure you can see it writhing. You have a vision of it exploding with a scurry of thousands of spiders, so you decide to give it a wide berth while you consider your next move. To the left is the door to the general surgery ward. You can hear a faint yet frenetic squeaking from inside, but if you want to enter, turn to **45**. The orthopaedic ward is on your right (turn to **65**) but if you'd rather, you could continue along the passageway (turn to **159**).

62

The door swings open and you stride through into the darkened corridor. Do you have any crushed sea eagle talons in your possession?

Yes	Turn to **375**
No	Turn to **98**

63

And you call yourself a healthcare professional. What were you thinking? There might be 12 *pairs* of ribs but that's not the number of ribs, is it? You close the fridge door and head to the storage area, not at all in control of your body. You are simply a puppet now and can only watch as your hands insert the cannula into a vein, then start a formaldehyde infusion. With wide, staring eyes, you watch the embalming fluid enter your body, feeling an incredible pain wrack your insides. You die with the most gruesome expression on your face.

64

You aim towards the faint green glow and realise that you've gone through an archway in the cave wall. The humming is louder here and gradually, you realise that you're surrounded by refrigerators. All of them have the green LEDs indicating the temperature but one has a flashing red light. However, before you can even wonder what the problem is, a gentle voice emerges from the side of the room.

    'Did my mother send you?'

    'Who's there?' you ask.

    'Come closer, so we can talk,' the voice says.

If you think this could be a mistake, you can leave and head back to the passageway (turn to **270**) or you could do as you've been told and go closer (turn to **28**).

65

Expecting a true horror-style ominous creak from the door, you're surprised when it opens silently. The ward looks like it's been abandoned for a decade and suddenly, you're reminded of the ghost town created by Chernobyl. Is that what's happened? You rush to the windows to look out then wish you hadn't. All you can see is a thick, dense forest, encircling and encroaching on the hospital as if it regretted previously giving up that space and now wanted it back. Where was the carpark? The high-rise tower block? The dual carriageway?

'It's always like that. Wherever we go.'

You scream and whirl around, clutching your chest. The voice came from the far end of the ward, but you can't see anyone.

'You'll have to come closer. I can't move.'

As you go further into the ward, past the rusting bed frames, you can see that a curtain has been drawn around the last bed space.

'Is that you behind the curtain?'

'Yes, they shut me away from prying eyes. It's not pretty.'

Those last words freeze your hand, which was posed ready to pull back the fabric. You take a second to gather your nerve, then step through the parted curtains. Your first thought is that it isn't so bad. An ordinary looking woman lying prostate on the crumpled and blood-stained sheet, albeit with long scars over each limb. She smiles reassuringly at you and as you return the smile, you start to see how *flattened* she looks. Your smile becomes a grimace, when you circle the bottom of the bed and realise exactly what has happened to the woman.

'They're all mine,' she says, pointing with her eyes at the pile of bones on the floor. 'He took them all, even the skull, but they weren't the right ones.'

You stand with your fist pressed into your mouth, trying to suppress the urge to cry or vomit, which both threaten to make an appearance. Eventually, you realise that you really should do something, so do you try to reinsert the bones into her body (turn to **105**) or fetch her a glass of water (turn to **358**).

66

You duck and squeeze through the narrow doorway. From what you can see — white tiles and an ornate mahogany towel rail — it must be the bathroom. Since when did trainee nurses get *en suites*? You look up at the large mirror above the sink and see a scene from a nightmare reflected in it. A woman with a slit throat is stood behind you. You scream and clamp a hand over your mouth. Is that Nancy? The wound in her neck gapes horrifically, exposing the ridged windpipe, but now you can tell that it isn't Nancy. It's just another victim. How many have there been?

'Are you here to finish this?' she asks, the jaw movement tugging obscenely at the wound. It's a good question. The truth is that you just want to get out, but it's looking more and more likely that finishing this is what you have to do first. You nod.

'Good. I suppose it's not very charitable of me to want someone dead, but I was only 19. 19 and training to be a nurse. I just wanted to make my father proud but look at me. Dr Carmichael took my virtue then my life.'

'Can you help me?'

'All I know is that the right place to find him, is the obvious place to find a surgeon.'

You absorb her words then frown. That doesn't make sense! You started off in the operating theatres — that wasn't the right place, was it?

'Do I have to go back there?' you ask, feeling overwhelmed with desperation. After trying so hard to leave, did you now have to go back?

'Stop thinking about where you are and consider *when* you are. Now take *this* and go. Stay in one place too long and he'll find you.' She pushes you towards another door and shoves you back out into the corridor. You stand there stunned, and it takes a few seconds before you look at the object that the murdered nurse pushed into your hand. A **tiny brass key with the number 21** engraved on it. It must be important, so you put it into the bag and carry on along the corridor. Turn to **81**.

'No, I'm not here to take your blood. I'm here to give you medicine,' you say reassuringly, as you fetch a glass from the cupboard, put some water into it and stir in the aconite powder. It dissolves easily and you smile as you turn and offer it to the child. There is a moment's hesitation, but the girl takes the glass and swigs the entire contents. She wipes a hand across her mouth, winces as a sudden pain grips her stomach, then smiles at you.

'Jezebeth says that you are proving your worth. Well done.' Before you can reply though, the child grimaces in agony and a thick white foam issues from her mouth. Her eyes roll back and she collapses onto the gurney, contorting with spasms. In less than a minute, she is dead and as you watch, the body morphs into a Plasticine-like mass. No limbs or hair or even freckles — just putty waiting to be moulded and half-buried within this, lies something. You gingerly prise it out of the ooze. It is a deep and dazzling blue colour — a snake made up of articulated segments of Lapis Lazuli. It's beautiful but you also think it could be useful, so you wipe it as clean as possible on your scrubs then place it in the bag. You leave this room but where should you go now?

Right, heading back to the junction   Turn to **9**
Left, leaving the ward via the door   Turn to **62**

With your words, the crone smiles excitedly, looking almost like a child and fetches a small ornately designed wooden chest. She throws it to the floor in front of you, then squats down cross-legged, so the box is between you both. From a pocket, she pulls three keys and throws these next to the chest. Finally, she speaks.

'I am apparently number 1, but I will always be Erichtho. No one can take my name from me. This chest holds the answers you need but three keys must be inserted in the right order. Which two of my sisters have you met? Which numbers were they given when their powers were taken? If you know, you will prove yourself worthy.' She gives a small jerk of her head towards the keys. You examine them and realise that they have different numbers engraved in the bow. There is a key labelled 1; another is 3 and the last one is 2. The crone waits until you've looked at the keys, then says, 'The correct order from left to right is the number of the pineal gland, then the tongue and finally, teeth.' She leans back and closes her eyes. It's up to you now. What order do you put the keys in?

123
132
213
231
312
321

When you've decided, turn to the section with the same number as your chosen order.

69

Standing in the middle of the room, you can see two doors — one straight ahead and the other in the right-hand wall. The three figures wait in the corners and are, unsurprising, swathed in grey cloaks. You can see now that they are old women with long, grey hair and tightly shut eyes. You open your mouth, but before you can say anything, you hear someone speak.

'Come closer, stranger. I don't see so well, although it's better than my sisters.' The woman in the left-hand corner gives a callous cackle and beckons you. You go closer and see that she has only one eye, which is peering at you with a bloodshot intensity. You realise now that the two other women are not sleeping, but their eyelids are sunken into the empty sockets underneath. Are they more victims?

'You are in a perilous place, my dear, but my friend tells me I should give you a chance to escape.' She gestures to the fourth corner and you turn and see a large frog sitting placidly there. You notice too, that the door you came in through has disappeared. There is no way back. The frog makes a strange throaty gurgle and you turn back to the one-eyed woman. If you want to tear down the tapestry to find an exit, turn to **279**, but if you'd rather attack the frog, turn to **148**. Maybe though, you should just hear her offer (turn to **361**).

70

You step back into the green, sludgy water and think about where to go now. You can either go back towards the A&E unit (turn to **146**) or left, following the corridor to the other sections of the hospital (turn to **135**).

71

You carry on, step by step, except... Shouldn't you be at the bottom by now? At 100 steps, you have to accept that this is not normal. In the pitch-black, you turn around and start climbing again, desperation mounting. Where's the door out of here? At 200, your thighs are aching but the stairs don't end. Maybe you shouldn't have given up when you were going down? Maybe the ground floor exit was just a few steps away? You turn around and start heading back down again. At least that's easier on the legs. At 500, you slump onto the step and sob gently. There is no way out. You realise that now. Perhaps the next person who's brought into this chaos will find your skeleton, curled up in the foetal position, and will wonder whatever happened to them.

72

Despite what you're about to do, you feel a real sense of peace. This means you're getting closer to going home. Carmichael continues to gasp and choke and although you recognise that the end is near, you want to make sure. You grab his hair with your left hand and draw the knife swiftly through his throat. You keep on sawing until the head is free, then you raise it up, staring into the dead eyes. Showing more respect than he ever did to his victims, you place the head on his chest then go towards the narrow stairs between the gallery pews. Turn to **394**.

73

You're a bit jarred but nothing's broken. Still, that's not much comfort as the pit is far too deep for you to get out of. The sides are smooth concrete — no foot holds, no ladders, nothing. Just over the rim, you can see the door to the Children's Ward and through its tiny window, you see the blush-pink light inside. You crouch down on your haunches, trying not to cry but feeling so helpless. In the midst of this though, there is a nagging thought and eventually, you get it. The pink light! Have you found anything that also had a pink glow? There may be a connection, you never know. After all, if the alternative is staying in the pit, it's got to be worth a try, hasn't it? What do you fetch from your bag? A white handled knife (turn to **104**) or crushed sea eagle talons (turn to **325**)?

74

You think this is where the Crow told you to go but it spoke so quickly, you're not really sure. After a couple more steps, you spot a heap of dried leaves on the floor and have an overwhelming compulsion to pick them up. You see your hand raise the debris and stuff it down your own throat. You start to cough, but you've already picked up more and are using both hands to pack it all in. Your fingers probe deep at the back of your mouth, making sure that every available space is blocked. You can't breathe, your lungs are burning, and your vision is blurry at the edges, but you can't stop. It's as though someone else is controlling your body. Luckily, death will come soon, giving you little time to wonder what went wrong.

You hesitantly open the door, fully expecting to hear alarms and shouting. Instead, there is silence and the overwhelming perfume of flowers. For a second, your airways tighten with the rush of pollen, but then you relax and take in the sight. There are some machines and lead gowns hung up on the wall, but it's difficult to see them beyond the thick carpet of lilacs that covers the floor and somehow, drapes up the walls and over the furniture. The air is heavy with their scent but it's a peaceful, dreamlike atmosphere. Suddenly, there is a slight movement; a shifting of the pale purple petals and then the woman sits up. The flowers tumble off her and she looks around, although you can see that she has no eyes. The eyelids are sunken inwards with just a darkness where the orbits should be. You guess that this is another of Carmichael's victims.

'I'm here,' you say, trying to be helpful. She smiles gently and indulgently.

'I know where you are. I see things. I divine. I know where you've been, and I know where you might go. My eyes may be gone but thanks to the lilacs, I still have my power. I was number 11 but as you bested the tyrant, my name is restored. I am Magda and my sisters and I will be forever grateful to you.'

For a few seconds, you don't know what to say. It's been the longest nightshift and you're in danger of succumbing to your weariness, but from somewhere, you find fresh strength.

'You know where I *might* go in the future?' you ask. She smiles again.

'There are so many different choices that you can make. I cannot predict where your free will takes you, even though my vision penetrates over distance and through time.'

Ah, now you know why the red light was lit up! As you're thinking of what else you could learn from her, your eyes roam around the room. In the corner, on top of what looks to be a filing cabinet, there is a scarlet flower. Just one single, solitary scarlet flower in the sea of lilacs.

'So you've noticed the Pimpernel? Take it,' she instructs. However, this would mean ploughing through the flowers. If you're willing to do this, turn to **142**. If you'd rather not, you can try to steer the conversation in a different direction (turn to **102**).

76

You say the name, but the lab technician simply rubs a hand over his blue-grey chin and shakes his head. He stares past your shoulder at the wall for a long time, then turns and heads back up the stairs.

'Stop. Please,' you cry, but he ignores you. He doesn't even look back; he just says, 'You know nothing. No one can help you here.' It seems pointless to follow him, so instead, you decide to carry on down the stairs. Turn to **222**.

77

You grab the parchment from your sock and re-read it. You thought that Pendle must be a man and you were looking for his wife but no! It was referring to Pendle *Hill*, so this must be one of the Lancashire Witches.

'Allow me to introduce myself,' she says politely. 'My name is Alice and I can tell you that the Athame knife is hidden within a mirror. You must be wise to be able to reach it, but Nathanael can guide you. Ask him for advice and you will take the knife.' With that, she gives a slight bow of the head and leaves the room. You think about following her, but you can tell from the absolute silence that she has disappeared. You've had enough of the damp stench in this room, so you hobble out too. Turn to **368**.

78

You nervously open the door and peer around. It's just a corridor with oak-panelling, a faded burgundy carpet and a few oil lamps to light the way. So far, so good. You reach the end and panic for a second, as you realise that there's no exit. Suddenly, there's a ratcheting noise as cogs turn and the panel in front of you is raised like a portcullis. You look behind and see that the other door has now vanished. There's nothing else for it then. You duck down and go into the next room. Turn to **308**.

As you walk to the other end of the laundry, you remember the photograph clutched in your hand. It's a small, old-fashioned and yellowing print, but when you turn it over, you're shocked to see the image. It's you! What? How? When? You realise that it was probably taken last night — was that really just last night? — when you were asleep in the break room. You stare at the impossible photo and wonder if the washerwoman could help again, but she seems to have vanished. Oh well, nothing to be gained from standing here all day. You try to put the photo in your pocket, but they are getting quite full now and you don't want to crumple it. All around you are piles of freshly laundered sheets and you notice a spare cotton bag. Perfect. You grab it and swing it over your shoulder, then transfer all the things that you've collected so far into it. That's better. You carry on to the far end and leave the laundry room, finding yourself in a long corridor adorned on each side by oil paintings. They are mostly landscapes and portraits of Victorian dignitaries, but amongst them, there is a gothic rendition of a dark demon crouched on the chest of a sleeping child.

If this reminds you of a name, turn to **160**; if not, you continue until you reach a crossroads (turn to **216**).

80

'Correct!' they say jubilantly and beckon you over to them. You sit down cross-legged and smile reassuring at the children. They look at you, then at each other and then back to you. After an eternity, one of them says, 'We were arguing about the colour of smoke needed to destroy a demon. I say it should be the banishing colour.'

'But I say it should be the purifying colour,' interjects the other. You look at their serious expressions and reply, 'Well, both of you can't be right, so one of you must be wrong.' The children shake their heads in unison and say, 'Not wrong. Just falsehoods. The question is: Do you know who's lying?'
If you know of a way to test whether someone is telling the truth, now would be a good time to practice it. If not, you may have to guess later on but that's better than nothing. The children go back to bickering over their bridge-building, having lost all interest in you. You get up and leave them to it (turn to **398**).

81

At the end of the corridor, there is a sharp turn to the left, shortly followed by yet another left turn, but before you take it, you hear voices and the unmistakable sound of footsteps climbing up a staircase. Whoever it is, they're coming towards you. If you decide to go around the corner and take them by surprise, turn to **344**. If you'd rather stay hidden, turn to **154**.

82

Before it even happens, you know it's gone wrong. You can just sense the shifting in the atmosphere. You'll never know though, that the silver chalice was the correct vessel and the blood had to be from the puppet master, which meant you should've drained the uterus. You'll never know because the finest stretched wire whips across the room and slices through your neck. For a few seconds, your head rests there with a stunned expression before toppling off onto the floor. You were so close, yet so far.

83

You vaguely remember that Joseph Lister was famous in medical history but what for? Maybe if you knew that, it could lead you to some other answers. You look desperately around the Recovery area, hoping for inspiration but there's not a lot here. Eventually, you think you've remembered what Lister was best known for, so what do you go to look at?

> The bottle of antiseptic soap   Turn to **307**
> The box of face masks   Turn to **264**
> The ECG monitor and leads   Turn to **175**

84

You crouch down next to Samael's chair, keeping a close eye on that hand — he'd better not smear shit over you!

'Hello sir,' you say, thinking politeness may help. 'Have you anything you can tell me?' The old man's eyes don't focus or shift, but he smiles and mutters, 'Make sure you visit the physiotherapy room. You will learn something from Jinny there.' With that effort, his face collapses again into an inanimate state, so you stand and leave the day room (turn to **201**).

85

You say the word 'Glossal' and wait for a thunderclap or something equally dramatic.

'What *are* you doing?' The Crow asks, head tilted to one side. Feeling slightly stupid, you sit down, cross-legged on the floor in front of it.

'I was told that you know the way to get out of here.'

'Indeed, I do. Well, out of this part, anyhow. When you leave this part, you'll be in another part and that part is a very different kettle of fish, I assure you.'

'Do you know how to get out of *that* part?' you ask, tentatively.

'Oh no. That part is *his* part. Or is it her part? I'm not party to that part. All I've heard is that Jezebeth is important in that part.'

You pause and think about your next question. The Crow seems to be quite tetchy and you get the feeling that if you upset it, that'll be that! What should you ask?

Can Jezebeth help me?   Turn to **19**
Where is the exit?   Turn to **250**

86

You stride around the operating table, keeping one eye on this man/demon and the knife raised. You will obliterate the name, but which one do you scratch out?

Carmichael	Turn to **360**
Jezebeth	Turn to **290**

87

Being on the floor, you are disadvantaged, and he knows it. He smirks, then bolts forward. You try to leap away, but stumble. You fall inches away from him and know that you can't escape. He raises the blade and then you cough. It comes from nowhere and with no warning, but you cough and a cloud of grey ash is ejected from your mouth. It engulfs him and instantly, he starts clawing at his throat. The cremains pour into his mouth, choking and suffocating him, as the burnt witches finally take their revenge. After a few minutes, he lies dead in front of you, a ghastly grimace fixed on his face, but before you can start to process what's just happened, you sense another presence in the room. Jezebeth has arrived. Turn to **313**.

88

You fetch the candle from the bag but then realise you have no way of lighting it. After all, if you had matches, you wouldn't have been stumbling around this pitch-black cave in the first place. But maybe there is a way of creating a flame — have you been told of a Goddess to call upon if you ever found yourself in this very situation? Now would be a good time to follow the advice, but who do you call?

Amphitrite	Turn to **111**
Gaea	Turn to **275**
Hestia	Turn to **221**

89

There is a moment of pure fear as you swing onto the ladder, but it's secure and easily holds your weight, so you start a steady descent. At first, you think the ladder is made of branches knotted into the rope but on closer inspection, you suspect they're actually bones — femurs, to be precise. You blank it out and carry on, certain that you'll get to the bottom soon. Twelve minutes later, you finally see a dull light and realise you're about to drop through a ceiling, into a room. But which room? Oh great, you think, as you start to see familiar looking items. The mortuary. Turn to **253**.

90

You are shocked by what you see, because a young girl with red plaited hair and freckles is sat on the gurney, her legs swinging.

'You look confused. Have you come to take my blood?' asks the child, but you don't answer. You can clearly see that there's nowhere for the doppelgänger to hide in here, which can only mean one thing. Whatever it is, it has the power to mimic forms and now, it's pretending to be this child. There's only one thing you know about so far that would want to trick you! This has to be Jezebeth's work. You take a step back and consider your options. You could try to get away before anything bad can happen (turn to **285**), however, if Hecate gave you a powder, you could use that. She said that it had two names: one was Carmichael's Monkshood and the other was…? If you know what the powder was called, turn the name into a number by using the code: A=1, B=2, C=3 ….. Z=26. Add the numbers together and turn to the section with the same number.

91

You pluck your trusty biro out of the scrubs pocket and scribble in the missing letters P and R. As you turn the page, an advert catches your eye. It's a Victorian man complete with stovepipe hat and extravagant moustache, but his entire body is a carrot. Apparently, this is meant to entice you to buy seeds. You raise your eyebrows at how bizarre it is. The rest of the newspaper is just more adverts, obituaries and local stories, and you can't escape the fact that you're now prevaricating. With a sigh, you put the newspaper down and instantly it becomes engulfed in a golden flame. You gasp, leaping onto your feet, away from the burning mass. Soon, all that remains are the black wisps of paper, which float slowly down like snowflakes. You can now leave the department either by the way you entered (turn to **17**) or the opposite exit (turn to **208**), or if you haven't yet tried the door with the red warning light and would like to do so, turn to **75**.

92

You rattle the small pewter bell and its delicate tinkling sound can barely be heard in the pharmacy. Feeling stupid, you put it down on the counter with a tinny clatter and contemplate giving a bellow of 'Jezebeth' — maybe just shouting the demon's name will work — but then you sense a shifting in the atmosphere and turn around to face this presence. Jezebeth has arrived. Turn to **313**.

After a few more steps, you reach stairwell B and see that the fire door has got something daubed on it. It's gloomy here, so you have to rely on the weak glow of your trusty pen-torch. Still, there's no hiding what this symbol is. You curse and feel tears spring to your eyes. Not that you believe all that superstitious nonsense but

 really? A five-pointed star! What's it called? A pentacle! That's never a good sign. You try the door but surprisingly, it won't shift. It's locked, so you walk on to the end of the corridor, which turns sharply to the right. If you choose to follow the corridor around, turn to **2**, however, straight in front of you are the doors to the Renal Unit and if you want to investigate there, turn to **215**.

94

'The answer is WILLOW.' At first, you think that you were wrong because nothing seems to happen, but as you study the mirror, you realise that the reflected image is not quite as it should be. You can see a small box by your feet, so you crouch down and grope around for it, keeping your eyes glued to the mirror. Although you can *see* your hand touching the box, you can't *feel* it. There's no explanation other than the box exists only on the other side of the mirror. Do you want to try to go through the mirror to retrieve the box? If so, turn to **331**. If not, you can either go and look at the statue (turn to **244**) or go through the double doors (turn to **41**).

95

Whilst you stare, half-mesmerised by the intestines, a flash of inspiration hits and you shout, 'When I'm small, I'm the longest. When I'm large, I'm the shortest. What am I? THE SMALL AND LARGE INTESTINES!' But your moment of triumph doesn't last long. You're rewarded by a flurry of scrambling from underneath the bed, which makes you instantly regret being so loud, but it's not an avalanche of rodents. The floor itself is starting to crumble. A tiny patch to start with but the hole grows and spreads wider, the particles of floor now seeping down like sand grains in an egg-timer. You shuffle back away from the edge but, as quickly as it began, it stops. You edge forward cautiously and look down the hole. What the…? It's a spiral staircase.

If you want to descend the stairs, turn to **397**. If you wish to just leave this ward and go back to the thoroughfare, turn to **362**.

96

Charpentier gives an upward nod of his head, then starts wiping the paw over his cheek.

'Then I wish you good luck. I have told you all I know and can be of no further help to you. If you could close the door on your way out, I'd be very grateful.' He continues with his grooming, making it clear that the conversation is over. You leave the room, closing the door, as instructed. Turn to **126**.

97

You yank the door handle down and pull desperately but it's locked fast. A shadow looms over and you turn, screaming. You put your hands up, but he is too strong and the knife is too sharp. Mercifully, darkness takes you and your end is over quickly.

98

In the gloom, you can just about see that the corridor soon takes a turn to the left but there are no signs saying where it leads to. Oh well, you'll just have to…
Without warning, the floor disappears from under your feet and you hurtle straight down. After a few seconds of shocked and stunned immobility, you examine yourself for injury. It could've been worse — you'll have a bruise or two but luckily, nothing is broken. You turn your attention to the pit and feel a dread settle in your stomach. It's deep and the smooth concrete walls have no footholds and definitely no ladder! You shake your head in disbelief. It can't end like this, stuck in a pit and dying of thirst! But sometimes, that's just the way it goes.

99

Back in the small dingy foyer, you look around and weigh up your options. Where do you go now?

Toilet	Turn to **195**
Furnace	Turn to **219**
Mortuary	Turn to **6**

'You are kind,' she replies, 'but it is long gone now. And it wasn't a child anyway.' You look quizzical but dread to find out what she means by that. She pats your hand, as if sensing your unease.

'I am the puppet master,' she states. 'With my marionettes, I could control a person. Pull their strings, you could say. I was trying to take hold of that monster Carmichael, but he ripped the puppet out before it was ready. And then he took my power to ever try again. You killed him?' You nod. 'You need to destroy Jezebeth too. You know that?' You nod again. 'You will need access to her secret room. When you find yourself in the apothecary, examine the laudanum.'

With that, she gives a painful cough, which disturbs the contents of her abdomen. The disgruntled and swirling black mass rises up, buzzing in your face. By the time, they have settled back down to continue their feast, Gretl is no longer with you. When you think you are in the location that Gretl has told you, **multiply that section number by 10** and turn to the new section. For now though, you can either leave the delivery room and head further along the corridor (turn to **119**) or you could investigate the ajar door (turn to **53**).

101

You turn around, ready to face whatever is there. A stocky, middle-aged man with dark sideburns and a moustache is stood between the operating table and a blackboard. Although you think you know who this is, you see 'Carmichael Jezebeth' scrawled on the board in chalk. For a few seconds, you stare at each other but then surprisingly, he smiles.

'My final witch,' he claims warmly. 'I have waited so long for you and your power.'

'I'm not a witch,' you stutter, 'I'm a nurse. I have no power. I just want to go home.' Your words have no effect though — he simply shakes his head indulgently.

'Exactly. My nurse witch with her healing hands. Soon to be *my* hands.'

The blood drains from your head as you realise what he's saying, but a burst of adrenalin courses through you. *Not bloody likely*, you think.

'There's no way you're cutting my hands off!' and you draw the Athame knife from your bag. Now, it's his turn to look frightened but that only lasts a few seconds, then a scowl settles on his face.

'What do you intend to do with that?' he asks. It's a good question. What *are* you going to do with the knife?

Cut his throat from ear to ear   Turn to **378**
Scratch his name from the blackboard Turn to **86**

You know that the Scarlet Pimpernel is a character who hid a secret identity, so who knows what this witch could be hiding? It could be a trap set up by Jezebeth! You decide that you should try to get some useful information out of her, so you ask, 'Where should I go to from here?' The witch bows her head slightly then says, 'Go to the place of pain and joy. Of new beginnings and sometimes endings.'

You thank the witch for this advice, but she is already sinking back down under her eiderdown of lilacs. You wish that you could stay longer in this peaceful haven, but you can't, so you leave the room. Turn to **248**.

You have to lean in to reach the back of the furnace and can't help but envisage the Witch in Hansel and Gretel trying to bundle you into an oven, so you concentrate on rummaging around in the fine ash as a way to keep a lid on your rising hysteria. Suddenly, there's a small explosion, which sounds as if something's *sneezed* in the furnace, and you inhale a lungful of carbonised flesh and bone. You pull out of the furnace instantly, but no amount of coughing and spitting can remove the ash. You're regretting ever having the idea of checking out the furnaces when a noise from behind startles you. Turn to **121**.

104

You pluck the white-handled knife from the depths of the bag and wield it dramatically in front of you. Nothing happens. You shake it authoritatively high in the air and think about saying something, but what can you say? Eventually, you give up, sit down on the floor and examine the knife closely. It has green gunk pressed into its blade and for a second, you wonder if that could be the key. Hoping beyond hope, you sniff it and realise that it's crushed basil. It's just a kitchen knife and it definitely isn't going to get you out of the pit. Still, it might come in handy if you tire of waiting to die of thirst here.

105

You quickly assess the situation and think it would be best to start with the long leg bones. You start looking through the pile, gently placing the pelvis to one side, and just when you find the left femur, there is gut-wrenching scream of anguish. You look up to see the woman in pure agony and rush to her side.

'What's wrong? What can I do?'

'Don't touch them,' she manages to cry out. 'The bones were cursed the second they were removed. *I* was cursed to stay like this for ever, or at least, until he is finally dead.'

'He? Who's he?' but you are interrupted by the sight of every single bone now crumbling into a fine, white powder. The woman weeps, tears rolling down her face, then she closes her eyes and will not, or cannot, speak any more. You wonder if the pain was too much — have you killed her? But without the sternum, you can clearly see a pumping heart in her chest and know that she lives on. There's nothing more you can do here and frankly, you've done enough damage, so you leave the ward. Turn to **30**.

106

The dim light flickers constantly, making the shadows jump and shift. You keep seeing figures out of the corner of your eye, but when you look, there's nothing there. On your left are the doors that lead back to the ITU — well, no point going there, you think — but now something else has got your attention. Turn to **93**.

107

The room is dark and dank and the dripping noise is coming from a leaky tap in the corner. There is a small window high in the far wall but bars and dirt prevent any sunlight from penetrating the shadows. A sturdy, wooden chair faces you, with numerous leather straps attached to it, and you presume that whoever sat in the chair was doing so involuntarily. The reason for that becomes clearer as you look at the tall, wooden barrier behind it with a ladder and two buckets. What was meant to be therapy was, in fact, torture. You can picture the frightened, naked person struggling against the restraints as bucket after bucket of cold water was thrown over them, and you shiver in sympathy.

Although it's a bit gruesome, you are weary so you decide to sit in the chair until you regain some strength.

You're not sure if you've fallen asleep but suddenly, you sit bolt upright, certain that you've just heard a noise behind you. Do you stand on the chair and peer over the barrier (turn to **193**) or pretend to still be asleep (turn to **283**)?

108

The foyer is carpeted with a huge Persian rug and there are ornately carved oaken double doors directly ahead but you're not sure where they lead to. Somewhere important, maybe? On the left side of the foyer is a huge mirror in a gilded Baroque frame and on the right, stands a full-size marble statue of a man in Puritan-style clothing. If you go directly through the double doors, turn to **41**, however, you could first examine the mirror (turn to **386**) or inspect the statue (turn to **244**).

109

You grasp the shiny black amulet and thrust it towards Jezebeth. For a moment, her face is like a mask, devoid of emotion and you begin to hope that maybe, just maybe, this is the answer. But then she smiles and you know that all is lost. That was your last throw of the dice and you failed. The creeping sensation continues throughout your body. It's like someone is putting on a new outfit, stretching themselves into each and every nook and cranny. Finally, she takes you over and at least now, you stop thinking about all the agonising things that Jezebeth can do to you. You simply stop thinking.

110

You say the name, but the lab technician simply rubs a hand over his blue-grey chin and shakes his head. He stares past your shoulder at the wall for a long time, then turns and heads back up the stairs.

'Stop. Please,' you cry, but he ignores you. He doesn't even look back; he just says, 'You know nothing. No one can help you here.' It seems pointless to follow him, so instead, you decide to carry on down the stairs. Turn to **222**.

111

Holding the candle high in the air and panicking as the noise from above becomes more agitated, you whisper the name Amphitrite. Nothing happens. You say it again, a little louder but not too loud, just in case… But nothing happens. You wait and then throw the candle back into the bag. Fat load of use that was! You carry on walking, hoping that whatever is moving around up there, stays up there. Turn to **317**.

112

You push open the door and are almost blinded. For a second, you think it's just sunlight, but when your eyes finally adjust, you realise that the walls are painted a vivid yellow and you're not alone anymore. There is a young nurse sat in one of the chairs and opposite her are three elderly men. You approach the nurse but before you can ask her anything, she simply wags her finger at you.

'You may speak with one but only one of these fine gentlemen. Make your choice. There is Samael, Nathanael and Daniel.'

There's not much to tempt you with any of them. Samael seems to be concertedly rolling a small piece of excrement between his fingers; Nathanael is wearing urine-soaked pyjamas and Daniel has an impressively long string of drool hanging from his mouth. You consider your options.

Talk with Samael	Turn to **84**
Talk with Nathanael	Turn to **294**
Talk with Daniel	Turn to **385**
Leave the day room	Turn to **201**

113

A little further on, the corridor branches. Going straight on normally takes you to the medical wards but it seems to be blocked off with some strange barrier. The right turn should take you to another stairwell and more surgical wards. Where would you like to go now?

Straight on	Turn to **202**
Right	Turn to **125**

114

You walk down this corridor, past a short staircase on the right. The steps head down towards the lower level, which looks far too much like a dungeon for your liking, so you carry on. Eventually, you reach a door and its small sign states that you've arrived at the Sleep Disorders Laboratory, but the flamboyant and flowery declaration above the door is 'Welcome to Poppy Ward'. Poppy? Really? You open the door (turn to **223**).

115

You walk along the narrow corridor, exiting the x-ray department and stepping back into daylight. There are dark clouds gathering now though; maybe a storm is brewing. Ahead of you, the corridor takes a sharp turn right. You could take it at a quick run and if there's anyone there, you'd take them by surprise (turn to **214**) or you could take it slowly in case someone's laid a trap for you (turn to **300**).

116

You stand on tiptoes and reach into the dusty hole. Your fingers immediately find a roll of paper, which you grasp and pull out. Do you want to see if there's anything else in the hole?

| Yes | Turn to **259** |
| No | Turn to **367** |

The silvery moon casts a cold light around the large room. Normally, it was full of patients waking up after their operations, but now it's cluttered with discarded equipment and everything has a heavy coating of dust and mould. There's nothing here, you decide, but just when you set off for the exit, the ceiling lights flash on and off. You wait, not breathing, half-hoping, half-dreading that something else happens. Suddenly, it does. The wall light opposite switches on and then swings round, sweeping an arc of light across the room. If you've seen this happen before, you should remember a name. The name of a surgeon or more accurately, a butcher. Turn the name into a number by using the code: A=1, B=2, C=3 ….. Z=26. Add the numbers together and turn to the section with the same number.

If you haven't come across a name, the strange light means nothing to you other than it's probably time to get out of the department. You head for the exit. Turn to **8**.

118

You look tentatively at the bottles — mescaline, dried mushrooms and absinthe — and are feeling tempted to take a sip of the green liquid, when a thought occurs to you. Could Jezebeth's secret room be close by? Just as you consider the possibility, the shelves seem to lurch and slide before your eyes. Your attempt to grab onto something to prevent the fall is futile, and by the time you hit the floor, you are already deeply unconscious. You will never know what happened then or how you ended up back at the start, but maybe next time, you won't make the same mistakes. Turn to **1**.

119

You continue down the corridor, although it feels more like a tunnel with the pages plastered all around and words everywhere you look. At the end, there is a door and although you're not sure what lies beyond, you can hear the faint sound of dogs barking. If you want to go through and investigate, turn to **228**, but if you'd rather just follow the corridor around to the left, turn to **301**.

120

Before long, you reach the exit door, but when you try to leave, the door won't budge. You push it three times and even thump it with your fist in frustration but facts are facts. The door is locked. You have no choice but to go back to the junction and head right, leaving the ward that way. Turn to **50**.

Standing between you and the door is a young girl. She is dripping wet with long strands of pond weed cascading over her head and shoulders. She has the grey pallor of the dead, but her eyes are bright red with ruptured blood vessels. You presume this is another victim of Carmichael.

'What did he take?' you ask in a stammering voice. The girl closes her eyes and sighs, as if the memory is still too painful.

'I am number 4 but before that, I was Agnes. He took my adrenal glands. They gave him the power to create fire and to mock me, he keeps me here, in a fiery red room with the furnaces.'

'But why are you wet?'

'They drown witches, don't they? Dunk them again and again until they confess or die. Have you ever been held under water until your lungs are bursting?' You shake your head. 'Can you imagine how terrified I was?' You nod. 'The adrenalin was pumping round my veins, the glands ripe, like dripping peaches. The best time to harvest them, he said. And of course, it meant that any fires I tried to start in defence were extinguished. I had nothing else to fight with.' With that, she turns slightly and raises up her soggy linen tunic, showing you the gaping wounds at the bottom of each side of the rib cage. They look painful and you can't help but think of her having to feel that forever more. After all, the dead don't heal.

'I'm going to try and stop this,' you say. Agnes bows her head with a grateful smile.

'You must be careful though. Carmichael is much more than a man now. When he acquired the teeth, something changed. *He* changed. I don't know exactly, I hear talk of a demon, but I think that he has two names now.'

'Is the other name Jezebeth?'

'That, I do not know but maybe I can help you in another way. If you ever need a flame to light your journey, call on Hestia' You give a quizzical tilt of your head, but Agnes merely looks tired and apologetic. 'I must go now; it takes up too much energy.' And with that, the water dripping from her becomes a deluge and she simply drains away. In twenty seconds, all that is left of her is a puddle on the red floor.

You head for the door, trying to memorise her advice, and leave the furnace room. Turn to **347**.

122

You head down the passageway past more cell-like rooms until you reach a heavy steel door. You try the handle, but it's locked. Bored now and feeling oppressed by this gloom, you head back to the junction and this time, take the left-hand corridor. Turn to **236**.

123

You put the last key into its lock and hold your breath. Turn to **15**.

124

The purest white smoke spirals up to the ceiling. Both you and Jezebeth watch it in stunned silence, but then you hear that mocking laughter again. The demon leers at you, licking a spindly tongue over one of its fangs and you realise that you made the wrong decision. You start to feel a strange sensation through your body, as Jezebeth begins to take control. The end can't be too far away but before that happens, you quickly think about all the items you've collected. Maybe one of these could be useful. If you select the amulet made of Lapis lazuli (turn to **371**), but if you opt for the one made of obsidian, (turn to **109**).

125

This linking corridor has no doors or rooms, so nothing can jump out at you here, but suddenly you hear a noise from above. A deliberate, creaking sound. And there it is again. And again. You're in no doubt that there's something above you. Something or someone walking above you but trying not to be heard. Except... you're already on the top floor, so what's hiding in the roof space? You take a deep breath and try not to think about that. If you start panicking, you're doomed. You exhale slowly and look around yourself. Where should you go now? The entrance to stairwell A is just on your left (turn to **323**), so you could head downstairs. Otherwise you can follow the corridor around to the right and investigate more wards (turn to **392**).

You step back into the corridor and weigh up your next move. You could take the corridor that goes straight ahead from the bedroom door (turn to **247**) or take the corridor going right (turn to **155**).

127

You walk down the corridor. Far from Intensive Care being the safe option you hoped for, all you can see is carnage. The sign: 'INTENSIVE CARE UNIT Please buzz for entrance' is lying twisted on the floor. The security doors that normally barred unauthorised visitors are swinging off their hinges, huge holes punched through, and beyond them, who knows? You tread carefully over the debris, wondering whether this is still a good idea.

If you want to creep on into the Intensive Care Unit, turn to **52**. If you decide to ring the buzzer, turn to **218**.

128

So far, each and every cot has a doll in it. They are old-fashioned, made of rigid plastic with matronly hairstyles. Some have got modern cannulas taped to their arms; others have got tubes tied to their mouth. It is disturbing to say the least. You reach the last incubator and stop suddenly. This one is empty of dolls and all medical paraphernalia but standing on the thin mattress is a golden goblet. You open the side door and pull it out. It's beautiful and well-crafted, so you decide to put it into your bag for safe keeping. What now? Leave and head back into the ivy-covered corridor (turn to **7**) or head to the other door (turn to **211**)?

129

Empusa nods in a serious fashion, then leans back and smiles at you. Is this all a joke to her, you wonder.

'There is no answer to that. Some of us only find our power when we need it. People would like to have the knowledge of their destiny but true power is about believing in ourselves even when we think we have nothing but ourselves to depend on.' Empusa lowers her head in an enigmatic and affected gesture. Really? Is that all she has? Cod-wisdom! You think about demanding more answers, but then decide that you've had enough. You turn back to the archway, but what do you do?

| Leave straight away | Turn to **255** |
| Examine the fridges | Turn to **303** |

130

After a few steps in this direction, you have a choice to make. Where should you go now?

Left	Turn to **74**
Right	Turn to **291**

131

You sink into the water, smiling with pleasure as the warmth envelops you. You tip back your head, letting your hair soak and it feels wonderful. Almost like being back in the womb and floating safely in a liquid cocoon. If you want to simply lean back in the pool and relax for a few more minutes, turn to **340**. If you're tempted to submerge yourself completely, turn to **272**.

132

You put the last key into its lock and hold your breath. Turn to **15**.

133

Carmichael continues to gasp and choke on the floor and you recognise that the end is near. You crouch down at his side and lean over, so that your face is only inches from his. You stay like this for a few minutes, just watching and waiting, until he gives a long shuddering sigh. You feel his breath being drawn into your body, a thought which half-repulses you but somehow, it feels right too. Carmichael is still now. It's over for him but if you ever need to use a dying breath, remember the codewords **CHEYNE STOKES**. You stand now and head for the narrow stairs between the gallery pews. Turn to **394**.

134

Your footsteps sound loud against the stone tiles and echo against the bare walls. Gas lamps flicker, casting ever-changing shadows that make you flinch and look behind yourself. Before long, you reach another junction. If you head right, the passageway soon ends in what looks like a prison door (turn to **322**) whereas if you head left, the passageway just takes you further along until you go around a corner (turn to **35**).

135

The wide thoroughfare stretches out ahead of you. You've walked this way many times as it links to the staff carpark but for most visitors, it's the way to get to the medical wards and the out-patients department. On the left, is the hospital shop and when you glance over, you gasp and freeze with shock. The door is wide open and there's a woman stood in the middle of the shop. She smiles and gestures for you to come in. As you stare, wondering whether this is safe or not, you notice another person — a frowning man behind the till. You can find out what the woman wants (turn to **363**) or speak with the angry man (turn to **287**), but if you think it would be wiser to just continue walking, turn to **260**.

136

You arrive back at the crossroads and can go straight ahead to the closed door if you haven't done so already (turn to **374**) or take a left and head towards the staircase (turn to **206**).

137

You think this is where the Crow told you to go but it spoke so quickly, you're not really sure. After a couple more steps, you spot a piece of glass on the floor and have an overwhelming compulsion to pick it up. You grasp it tightly in your hand, wincing as it slices the skin but are completely unable to let it go. Almost as if you are watching someone else, you see your own hand raise the shard and plunge it into your abdomen. You make a deep cut, then throw the glass aside and reach greedily through the wound. You grab a coil of slippery intestine; the pain is unimaginable, but you cannot stop yourself from dragging your own gut out. It's as though someone else is controlling your body. You pull and pull until you have completely eviscerated yourself and then lie there next to the steaming pile of offal. Death will come, but slowly, giving you plenty of time to wonder what went wrong.

138

You're not stupid! You run the tap first to see what the water is like and although you're expecting it to be rusty-brown and fetid, it's a clear, cold gush. You drink greedily, unaware until this very second just how dehydrated you were. It's refreshing and revitalising and when you've taken your fill, you wipe your chin and leave the room. Turn to **387**.

139

With nothing to block the venom already in your body, it spreads and takes control. You can only watch with horror, as you lift your own wrist to your mouth and start gnawing at the flesh. Jezebeth wants your hands and will take them by any means. Your teeth are not designed for this — it's going to be lengthy *and* agonising. Plenty of time for you to wish you could do things differently.

140

You step into the wide corridor, grimacing as a splash of thick, green pond water soaks into your socks. You wonder briefly why the water is here but not in the labs, then remember that nothing makes sense anymore. As far as you can see, the entire thoroughfare looks flooded and the air is heavy with a stagnant odour. In front of you, lies the door to the ground floor section of the operating theatres. It has a freshly painted symbol on it — an eight-spoked wheel.

You are drawn to it, so cross over, arm outstretched, but when you touch it, you realise that it's been drawn in blood. You wipe your fingers on your scrubs and try the doors, but they're locked. So, where to now? You could go left to the Accident and Emergency department (turn to **146**) or head right, towards the hospital entrance (turn to **256**).

141

You have to stand on your tiptoes to grasp the handle but before you can pull the door open, you hear a soft rustling noise from behind. You spin around and scream uncontrollably, sensing a warm wetness spread out down your thighs. The corpse is standing in front of you; the sheet pooled around its feet, exposing the split ribcage and the empty cavity. It staggers forward, arms outstretched. You could run but you can't. You can't even breathe, so great is your fear. Its hands encircle your neck, squeezing as it lifts you clean off the floor. You can hear it grunting with the effort, although, without lungs, you're not sure how it's doing that. The sad thing is you'll never find out.

142

With difficulty, you scramble through the flowers, then gently pluck the Scarlet Pimpernel. You carry it carefully back to her and she takes it without hesitation, pushing it into your hair above your ear. As a fashion accessory, it's not really your style but stranger things have happened, so you're happy to go along with it.

'The Scarlet Pimpernel will always determine the truth and if you are going to have any chance of resisting the Demon of Falsehoods, you will need the truth.'

When you need to decide who is telling the truth, you should **divide the section that you are at by 2**, then turn to the section with this number.

You thank the witch for her kindness and watch as she sinks back down under her eiderdown of lilacs. You wish that you could stay longer in this peaceful haven, but you can't, so you leave the room. Turn to **248**.

143

The purest white smoke spirals up to the ceiling. Both you and Jezebeth watch it in stunned silence, but then you hear that mocking laughter again. The demon leers at you, licking a spindly tongue over one of its fangs and you realise that you made the wrong decision. You start to feel a strange sensation through your body, as Jezebeth begins to take control.

'The wrong decision? Oh dearie, you made more than one!' She caws mockingly and knocks the receptacle out of your hands with a flick of her tail. So you tried but you failed. The creeping sensation continues throughout your body. It's like someone is putting on a new outfit, stretching themselves into each and every nook and cranny. Finally, she takes you over and at least now you stop thinking about all the agonising things that Jezebeth can do to you. You simply stop thinking.

144

The wood has warped over time, so the drawer sticks a little. When you do manage to pull it out, there's not much to see. A battered-looking pocket watch, a hair comb studded with mother-of-pearls and a silver ring with an iridescent white and blue gemstone. You're tempted to take it but... Decide whether you put the moonstone ring on or put it back where you found it, then you can either examine the suitcase (turn to **383**) or head over to the small door (turn to **66**).

145

It may have made you feel better at the time, but breaking the mural was the worst thing you could possibly have done. You destroyed the entity that could've helped you get out of here! There are always consequences for our actions and you are going to pay a very heavy price for yours. It's just a matter of time before he finds you and it won't be pretty when he does.

146

You arrive at the double doors leading to the A&E department. It has a strange orange light emanating from it, which makes you wonder whether this was a good idea after all. Still, you're here, so you might as well go in.

The reason for the orange glow is simple. The ceiling, floor and every wall are painted orange. You walk into the waiting room, footsteps echoing because there isn't a single piece of furniture. No curtains, no chairs, no gurneys — nothing to absorb the sound. Through the glass doors of the exit, you see a brick wall, so there's no way out and fighting back the disappointment, you turn 180° and walk out of the waiting room. The large patient area is to your right and is divided into Resuscitation, general treatment room and a quiet room for psychotic episodes. Where do you choose to go?

Resuscitation   Turn to **328**
General treatment room   Turn to **288**
Quiet room   Turn to **192**

147*

You open the oak panelled door and emerge into a blindingly bright corridor. For a few seconds, you can't see, so just reach out for the wall and wait, but finally, you realise that you're in a short glass corridor with the sun streaming in. You can see lawns, shrubs and mature trees through the windows and the green is refreshing after all that gloom. The corridor ends in a junction and as you look, a figure darts across, from right to left. You gasp and almost shout out but then remember that not everyone here is your friend. You can say that again, you reply to yourself. Still, it looked familiar with the blue scrubs… You pick up the pace and look left when you reach the T-junction but there's no one there. So you're left with a decision — do you want to go left at the junction (turn to **304**) or head right (turn to **237**)?

148

Without pausing to think, you race across the room and launch yourself at the large, mottled amphibian. You punch it but that doesn't seem to have an effect, so you grab it and try to pound it into the floor. The frog is remarkably passive as you attempt to kill it, which makes you wonder briefly on the wisdom of this manoeuvre. You don't seem to be getting anywhere with this strategy; not to mention just how breathless you are. At this crucial point, you remember that frogs often secrete toxins through their skin. You look down at your palms and the stringy mucus smeared over them and try to wipe your hands clean but it's too late. Your throat swells and a terrible heat starts to burn you up from the inside. You die a painful and frightening death while the frog merely flicks its tongue out occasionally.

149

The demon stands before you, swaying slightly from side to side on a thick serpent body. The scales are a dull taupe colour but with shimmering edges of amber. The torso and head are that of a skeleton, albeit one with dried and leathery flesh tightly gripping the bones underneath. Her eyes are huge black holes and the jaw contains fiercely sharp snake fangs. A voice fills your head, although you don't see Jezebeth mouthing any words. You are practically numb with fear, listening to the confident and condescending laugh as the demon appraises you. If you have a snake bite wound on your hand, turn to **243**, but if you haven't, turn to **395**.

150

You place the wooden bowl on the table and take a deep breath. This is really happening. If you can do this right, you just might make it home. You feel a little trickle of sweat weave down your temple, then you pull the photo out of the bag. You have no idea how the image of you ended up in the mortuary, but it must mean something. You are the executioner, after all, so with a decisive move, you crumple up the photo and stuff it into the bowl. Next, you're going to mix it with some blood. If you have a recipe of this spell, you should know where to take the blood from; if not, you'll just have to guess and keep your fingers crossed. Which organ do you squeeze until the blood drips into the bowl?

The heart   Turn to **82**

The uterus   Turn to **320**

151

You stand in the middle of the prayer room, surrounded by umber. If you saw the anagram ROAM OR PYRE, then you're sure that you're in the right place, but what happens now? Well, if you recorded the codeword SHARDS, you must immediately turn to **145**. If you didn't, you can carry on reading.

Your frustration rises and just when you're on the verge of throwing the chairs around and storming out, you notice a slight movement. You dart round to face it but face what? All you can see is the mural. The forest scene with a deer, a badger and …of course, a crow.

You watch closely and see another movement. And another. And you realise that the crow isn't a glass image anymore but a real, live bird. It struts nonchalantly over the carpet towards you and caws purposefully. Almost as if it wants to talk with you… If you've been told how to communicate with animals, you should know the secret word. Turn the word into a number by using the code: A=1, B=2, C=3 ….. Z=26. Add the numbers together and turn to the section with the same number. If you don't know the word, you are doomed to wander the hospital looking for a way out until you simply die or *he* finds you!

152
You bring your face down to the vessel, close your eyes, open your mouth and hope for the best. With a low, drawn-out moan, Carmichael's dying breath sidles out and in a heavy mist, settles over the other ingredients. For a second, nothing happens, but then a spark and a hot, dense flame erupt. You concentrate with all your might, willing the right coloured smoke to curl up from the blaze. Which colour do you want it to be?

White	Turn to **143**
Black	Turn to **54**

153

You walk forward cautiously, going in the direction of the trickling. It must be close; the smell is starting to burn your nostrils. Soon, you see a cupboard and inside it, you can make out a huge porcelain jar with 'Leeches' scrawled on its side. The white glaze is cracked and strong vinegar is streaming out. As you stare in confused disgust, you catch sight of some writing on the wall. You go over to it, squinting and crouching to see better. Is that what you think it is? Yes, it's an inscription. You have to tilt your head to read it.

"The deepest slumber sets us free. Future, past and secrets see. The inky fingers heal all ills. Yet others call it heresy."

What did that mean? 'The deepest slumber'? Was that death or just anaesthesia? You repeat the inscription until you've remembered it, then carry on. Turn to **370**.

154

You stand splayed against the wall, listening intently and ready to bolt if they get too close. It sounds like two young women and you presume they are nurses. They seem to be bickering about something and sound out of breath. The footsteps stop and the voices get louder.

'How many times have I told you? It's the white-handled knife to slit the throat. That's the *only* way to off him!'

'You just don't listen. You never listen. Everyone knows it's the black-handled knife to scratch out his name!'

With a few more huffs and tutting, the footsteps resume but soon become fainter, until you can hear them no more. After deliberating for half a minute, you peek around the corner. There is a long staircase descending in front of you but no sign of anyone. You can see no doors or corridors and have no idea where the women went, only that they went. You go down the staircase and end up at a locked door. Turn to **278**.

155

You leave the sleep lab and carry on along the straight corridor until you reach another door. It's the physiotherapy department although its alternative name is 'Foxglove Hall'. You enter and find yourself in a long passageway that has a swimming pool at the end. You can smell the chlorine and see the ripples of reflected sunlight on the walls. If you want to investigate the pool area, turn to **12**. If you want to go all the way back to the junction in the sleep laboratory and take the other corridor, turn to **247**.

You trudge through the tunnel for ages, as it twists and coils and leads to who knows where. Eventually though, you reach a dead end and just as a wave of claustrophobia is growing, you look up and see another trapdoor. You jump, catch the handle and pull. It opens easily and a rope dangles down. It's at times like these that you wish you had a rickety ladder! On your third attempt, you make it up and drag yourself gratefully out of the tunnel, then stop dead, a stunned expression on your face. Where has the witch sent you? There are thousands upon thousands of pieces of paper plastered onto the walls, ceiling and doors. All the windows have been papered over, blocking the light out, and on all these pages are the scribblings of millions of words. You step closer to read it, but you can't understand the language; come to think of it, you don't even recognise the alphabet. Sometimes, out of the corner of your eye, you see the odd sentence part: 'when fungi migrate', 'sycophantic leanings' and 'appears wholly consumed yet' but when you turn to examine it, the words metamorphose back into a foreign tongue. The air is musty, dusty and feels oppressive, but at the far end of the corridor, you see an abandoned, empty crib. This has to be the maternity unit then, and your suspicion is proved correct when you find a hidden door nearby with the sign: Delivery Room. If you want to enter the room, turn to **372**. If not, you should carry on along the corridor (turn to **119**).

157

You head decisively for the exit door. Time to explore what else was down here. After all, you didn't even know there was a basement and have never been down here before. You take only a few steps, then hear a noise from behind. You spin around and scream uncontrollably, sensing a warm wetness spread out down your thighs. The corpse is standing in front of you, the sheet pooled around its feet. It staggers forward, arms outstretched. You could run but you can't. You can't even breathe, so great is your fear. Its hands encircle your back, dragging you close. You can hear it grunting with the effort, although, without lungs, you're not sure how it's doing that. As it starts to feed on your flesh, pulling great chunks off and swallowing them whole, you're certain you can hear it mutter again and again, 'Praise be to Baigujing for this meal'.

158

You crouch down next to Samael's chair, keeping a close eye on that hand — he'd better not smear shit over you!

'Hello sir' you say, thinking politeness may help. 'Have you anything you can tell me?' The old man's eyes don't focus or shift, but with a smile he mutters, 'Make sure you visit the physiotherapy room. You will learn something from Jinny there.' With that effort, his face collapses again into an inanimate state, so you stand and leave the day room (turn to **315**).

159

You reach the corner where the corridor goes around to the left, but directly ahead of you is the entrance to stairwell A. This means that you could go downstairs (turn to **323**), but if you'd prefer to stay on this floor and continue along the passageway (turn to **199**).

160

What name does it remind you of? It was some sort of animal, wasn't it? Was it mare (turn to **187**); mite (turn to **334**) or moth (turn to **174**)?

161

You look quickly around, then duck down behind the crash cart. Just in the nick of time too. You hear the far door slam open and the person scurry along the passageway. You press yourself into the wall, thinking if they come this way, they're bound to see you. Your luck holds though, and the person seems to go back on themselves. You hear a distant door open then close and breathe a sigh of relief. Whoever it was has entered one of the rooms near the far exit. You stand back up, then tentatively walk forward, but as you approach the junction in the middle of the ward, you pass a room and hear the soft voices of children from inside. Do you:

Enter the room?	Turn to **182**
Continue towards the far exit?	Turn to **273**
Go to the junction and turn right?	Turn to **50**

162

Just before you reach the main doors to the Intensive Care Unit, you hear a sound that chills your blood. A faint click as the connecting door to the operating theatres opens. You freeze. Footsteps again. Those heavy, confident footsteps but are they coming your way? There's nowhere to go if they do.

'You can run and you can hide, but all that do so have all died,' comes a sing-song voice from the distance. Not only is he hunting you, but he's taunting you too. Tears fill your eyes and trickle down your cheeks, but then you realise the footsteps are moving *away* from you, he's heading towards the rest of the hospital. You hear the door at the end open and close and you sag with relief. You're safe. For now.

You head quickly along to the junction. The door on your right, which leads back to the operating theatres, is now wide open and if you decide to go back there, turn to **332**. If you want to head left and follow in the man's footsteps, turn to **276**.

163

You walk down this corridor, past the short staircase where you left the psychiatric ward and carry on until you reach a door. The small sign states that this is the Sleep Disorders Laboratory, but the flamboyant and flowery declaration above the door is 'Welcome to Poppy Ward'. Poppy? Someone's quirky sense of humour, you suppose. You open the door (turn to **223**).

164

The storeroom is misleadingly named — it's a cupboard at best and an empty one at that. Out of annoyance with the whole situation, you kick the back wall and are amazed when it swings open. It's not a wall after all, it's a door! The darkness is impenetrable, so you have no idea what is back there. Do you want to investigate this mysterious space (turn to **245**) or just get out of there (turn to **99**)?

165

You exit the golden chamber and walk back down the panelled passageway to the pharmacy. You take your strange brew and carefully place it on the apothecary counter. There's no backing down now. It's time to face Jezebeth. If you possess a small pewter bell, turn to **92**. If not, turn to **381**.

166

You walk a short distance to the corner where the corridor turns left. You can either follow it around (turn to **61**) or investigate the Vascular ward, whose door is close by on your right (turn to **177**).

167

The door swings fully open, revealing an old-fashioned apothecary with three of the four walls dominated by oaken shelves filled with brown glass bottles of tinctures. Below these are hundreds of tiny wooden drawers concealing all manner of powders. In the middle of the room is a counter with delicate balancing scales and mortars. You stand there stunned, wondering what to do now, but before you can make a move, you sense another presence in the room. You turn, filled with dread, to face it. Turn to **249**.

168

You grasp the shiny black amulet and thrust it towards Jezebeth. For a moment, her face is like a mask, devoid of emotion and you begin to hope that maybe, just maybe, this is the answer. But then she smiles and you know that all is lost. That was your last throw of the dice and you failed. The creeping sensation continues throughout your body. It's like someone is putting on a new outfit, stretching themselves into each and every nook and cranny. Finally, she takes you over and at least now, you stop thinking about all the agonising things that Jezebeth can do to you. You simply stop thinking.

169

The figure gives a frustrated shake of its head, the beak hitting the side of the door frame. It grabs the crushed sea eagle talons from you and throws the petri dish far down the corridor. You turn to look where it lands and when you turn back, the door is already closing. You cry 'No! Wait' but it's too late. You've lost your chance to find the way out and now it's only a matter of time before *he* finds you.

The man meets you halfway and shakes your hand firmly, introducing himself as Cornelius. He seems trustworthy, so you let him lead you towards the woman, but she screeches and shuffles backwards. With some gentle words, Cornelius soothes her and she quietens, sitting with her arms clutched around her legs. Her forehead is resting on her knees and you can see clearly now that she has had the top of her skull removed. You point with a shaking finger at the wrinkled, exposed brain.

'What happened to her?' you ask.

'He calls her number 2, but she is Johanna. A powerful witch with a temper, but only with those who were cruel to others and did not heed her warning. She had a fierce ability to create madness and then *he* took it. I don't know how, but it was concentrated in the pineal gland, deep in the brain, and as you can see, he managed to gouge the gland out. Now all she can do is produce random chaos whenever she's frightened, so I stay with her. I protect her.' He smiles fondly at the witch and absent-mindedly strokes his wiry, white beard.

Before you can ask anything else, Johanna starts to rock back and forth and hit her fist against the jagged ridge of her skull. Abruptly, the shadows creep back and the room shifts with a kaleidoscope of colours. Cornelius pushes you to the door with a sharp 'Go!' and as you leave, you can hear him murmuring words of comfort to the ruined witch.

Back in the corridor, you can enter the prayer room if you've not already been there (turn to **11**). If you'd rather just carry on along the passageway, you can head left (turn to **113**) or right, which leads you back towards the operating theatre department (turn to **338**).

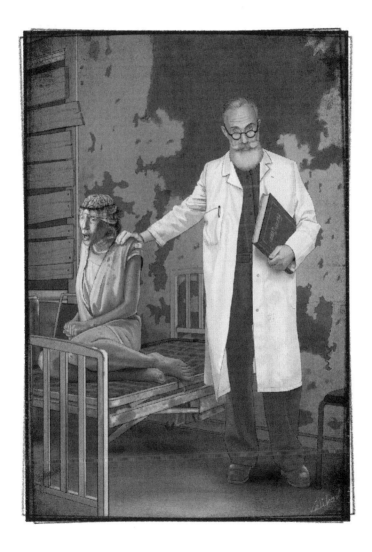

171

You exit the maternity department and step into another dark corridor; another tunnel, but this one is wrapped around with a thick carpet of ivy. Your feet sink between the tendrils and you can't help but think of these stems tightening around your ankles. You soon reach a door and the sign declares it to be the Special Care Baby Unit. If you want to enter (turn to **399**), but if you'd rather follow the ivy-covered corridor around the corner to the left (turn to **7**).

172

You leave the ward, noting that it was called 'Forget-Me-Not'. Considering that it seemed to be a geriatric ward, someone has a sick sense of humour, you think. You walk down a short corridor until you find yourself at a junction where another passageway leads off to the left. You could take this, even though you don't know where it leads to (turn to **333**) or you could just carry straight on (turn to **114**).

173

The microscope is antique and made of brass. You peer through the eyepiece and adjust the angle of the mirror. As it illuminates the field of view, you can see something moving, but it's blurred. You twiddle the focusing knob up and down. Is it some sort of insect? Those look like wings... At that moment, it comes into clear view. Oh.

You stand up and stare straight ahead, then bend back down. Yes, just as you thought — it's a fairy. So tiny and translucent with waves of different colours pulsing over its humanoid body. At first, you think that it's just randomly twitching around, but then you realise it's miming in an exaggerated fashion. Getting on its knees then leaning over and taking a deep breath in, before jumping up and repeating the entire thing again. Sometimes, you think that it's trying to talk, but you can't hear anything. It's just too small, you presume. As fascinating as this is though, you become aware that you've already spent a long time behind the mirror. It's time to get out!

You pick up the box again and put it under your arm, then taking a deep breath, push through the mirror.

Turn to **10**.

174

You whisper 'moth' and wait. Nothing. You say it more assertively. Nothing. You tilt your head back and proclaim it loudly. Nothing. You stare at the portrait and will something to happen, but… nothing. So you give up and feeling a bit stupid, head to the crossroads. Turn to **216**.

175

You start to examine the monitor and when you pull at the tangle of leads, something falls out. Your reflexes are sharp, so you catch a beautiful silver necklace with an oval jade pendant. Surely, this has some importance. You put it in your pocket for safe-keeping and head for the exit. Turn to **8**.

176

You delve into the bag, pulling out the sheets one by one and casting them onto the floor. Suddenly, your hand grasps something — not cloth or flesh but wood and string. You yank the object up, feeling it writhing and when it is finally revealed, you realise with a sinking heart, that it is a marionette. A puppet. Its carved face is angry, with a long protruding nose and rose-painted lips. It is also covered in blood, almost like it's just been born, then thrown away. Your instinct is to throw it away too, but when you try, you feel the strings wrap tighter around your wrist. You panic, making violent flicks of your arm to try and get it off, but it starts crawling up your arm towards your shoulder. Its little wooden mouth is twisted with fury and snarling, showing its tiny, pointed teeth. You try to grab it with your other hand, but it sinks those teeth into your fingers and with a frenzy, tears pieces of your flesh off. The pain is overwhelming, but luckily, the strings soon encircle your neck and start to pull tighter and tighter — your pain won't last for much longer.

177

Your hand grips the handle and is just about to turn it when you hear a cough from within. You freeze. The cough is followed by whistling — a chirpy little ditty — and heavy footsteps echoing around the ward.

He's in there! You tiptoe swiftly away along the corridor. Turn to **61**.

178

You push the door open slowly, braced to duck back and run, but the gust dies down and you realise where you are. The bright, whiteness of rows upon rows of freshly laundered and starched nurses' uniforms almost hurts your retinas and in the far corner by the open window, you see the reason for the noise. Hundreds of white cloth caps are flapping in the draught. For a second, the cleanliness and sunshine give you a welcome boost, but then the persistent doubts creep back in. Cloth caps? Nurses haven't worn those for… How long? A century? Maybe the question shouldn't be '*where* are you?' but rather '*when* are you?' You walk around the rows of dresses and see nothing but lawns and flower beds outside. It looks pretty but it definitely doesn't look like home. You decide to leave the room and on your way to the door, notice a beautiful, hand crafted, brown oak bowl. You put it in your bag and head back to the junction. You could choose now to go straight on (turn to **134**) or go right towards the staircase (turn to **206**).

179

As you get closer, you can see that the postcard is advertising some event to do with a Chemical Society. It has the ouroboros symbol emblazoned on it and you vaguely remember that it relates to the structure of benzene, but you can't imagine why the Intensive Care Unit would have this on such prominent display. Although you can't explain why you're so drawn to it, you pluck the postcard off the board and put it in your pocket. While you're here, you can check out the off-duty roster (turn to **292**) but otherwise, it's time to exit the unit (turn to **311**).

180

You wander between the tables, giving them an occasional shake to see if anything scuttles out from the rubbish, but other than a cascade of detritus, nothing happens. Against the far wall is the cashier's counter and you notice that the till is open. Curiosity gets the better of you and you cast an eye over. It's empty of money but you can see two items tucked into different compartments. One is an amulet, a figurine made of obsidian. The other is a bracelet made of braided snake's skin. Something tells you that it would be bad luck to steal both, but you feel compelled to take one item. Make a note of which one you steal.

If you haven't done so already and would like to investigate the Information Desk, turn to **239**. If you'd rather head back to the swampy corridor, turn to **70**.

Whether you genuinely don't have the book or you just didn't want to risk losing it, the round witch shakes her head sadly at your answer and says that she can't help you. As you start back up the rickety ladder, you hear her call out 'Good luck,' but her voice has such a tremor of doubt and despair in it, you wonder what awaits you. Still, you have nowhere else to go, so when you're back in the concrete corridor, you head for the door directly ahead. Turn to **167**.

182

You walk into the playroom and the children's voices instantly fall silent. For a second, you think that you must have imagined it and you're really alone, but when you look around, you see them. They're huddled together on the floor in the corner, hands gripping play bricks and a partially built bridge. One has jet black hair, black eyes and black skin; the other is like a negative — identical but snow-white. They look like chess pieces and both stare blankly at you. You don't feel a real sense of threat from them but they are unnerving. Just when you think that they're not going to speak, they ask, in unison,

'What are the medical prefixes for white and black?'

You think about this for a while and then you say that the answer is:

leuc and melan   Turn to **80**
lute and chrom   Turn to **364**

If you'd rather not play their game and get out while the going is good, turn to **398**.

183

With a gentle click, the lid of the chest springs open. The crone claps her hands together and sighs. Inside the chest, you see a single piece of paper, which looks as if it were torn out of a notebook. The handwriting is ornate and not easy to decipher in places. At first, you think it's just a recipe, but soon you realise that it's much more than that. It's the ingredients needed to destroy a demon.

> All placed in the silver cup
> The image of the executioner
> The blood from the organ of the puppet master
> A dying breath
> You will annihilate the demon if it burns with a smoke coloured…

'What's the last word? What's the colour?' you ask, waving the paper at Erichtho, but she's already started to feed on the corpse again and ignores all your entreaties. You have no choice but to give up and leave the room, tucking the paper safely in your bag for future reference. Turn to **227**.

'I mean no harm,' you announce in a trembling voice. 'I'm just trying to get home. Can you help me?' The thing regards you with a bored expression, unfolds one leg out, stretches it, then tucks it back underneath its rump.

'Excuse me,' you say with a less-trembling voice. Is this *thing* just going to ignore you? After a pregnant pause, it is obvious that, yes — it is just going to ignore you. You tut loudly then leave the room.

You can now choose to go to the general treatment area (turn to **288**) or the resuscitation room (turn to **328**), but if you've had enough of this place, you can simply leave A&E and go up the stairwell (turn to **357**).

The scabbed-over puncture marks throb and a watery liquid begins to ooze out, trickling down your fingers. Are you carrying a braided snake-skin bracelet?

Yes	Turn to **326**
No	Turn to **139**

You edge further into the second bay, following the strange sound. It gets louder as you get closer and then you can see the patient. The sheets have been kicked off and you can see its thin legs writhing. It's wearing a hospital gown, is just skin and bones and from its mouth, you can see the intubation tube. That's where the gurgling noise is coming from. Suddenly, it looks straight at you, eyes bulging and staring, then starts to pull at the tube. You dart forward, as if to help a normal patient but then you realise that the tube keeps coming. The patient gags and retches as it drags the tube from its throat, but it never ends — the tube just keeps coming. You stagger back with your hand over your mouth while it stares at you. There's definitely nothing that you can do to help it and if you've had enough of this place and *that* noise, turn to **311** to leave the Intensive Care Unit. If you can bear to stay a little longer and want to check out the room over on the far wall, turn to **23**.

187

You whisper 'mare' and wait. Nothing. You say it more assertively. Nothing. You tilt your head back and proclaim it loudly. Nothing. You stare at the portrait and will something to happen and, just when you're on the verge on giving up, the dark demon starts to move, stretching its neck from one side to the other, letting out a distinct crack. All of a sudden, you see the connection: mare = nightmare = bad dreams! Of course! Meanwhile, the demon is staring at you from the canvas. It looks bored.

'Are you ready?' it asks, in a tetchy voice. You nod apologetically.

'Take the straight-ahead option, up the stairs.'
You stand there, staring, waiting. It raises its eyebrows and regards you with a disbelieving expression.

'Are you an idiot?' For a second, you think that's a rhetorical question but then realise that it's waiting for an answer. You shake your head.

'So, take the straight-ahead option. Got it?' This time, you nod affirmatively. The demon rolls its eyes and sighs. The painting becomes a painting once more, and so you carry on until you reach the crossroads.
Turn to **216**.

188

You remember what the woman in the shop told you about being in a location that reminds you of her home city. She watched the Eiffel Tower grow, which means Paris and you're surrounded by Plaster of Paris. You feel confident, so you dip your finger into an opened bag and draw a large, white circle on the floor. You step over the line into the middle and say: 'Teeth and bones and brick-red flame; stand within the circle frame; line the passageway with string; give your thanks to Baigujing.' You stand there expectantly, but nothing happens — maybe you pronounced the name wrong — then suddenly, the wall in front of you starts to concertina apart. You can see what appears to be a shaft behind and you go to investigate. Looking down the deep, dark hole, you can see a rope ladder. Is this the string lining the passageway? If you want to try it out, turn to **89**. If you'd rather do anything other than go down a pitch-black hole, you can leave the department and head up the stairs (turn to **357**) or if you haven't done so already, you could go to the resuscitation room (turn to **328**) or the quiet room (turn to **192**).

189

You go back past the chairs and the door with the red warning light above it until you reach a junction. You can either turn left and head towards the Children's Ward (turn to **115**) or go straight ahead towards the exit (turn to **354**).

You walk into the huge room that was once the Renal Unit but now, strangely, seems to be a greenhouse. The air is filled with a heady, sweet smell of scent and all you can now hear is the continuous humming of thousands of bees. Huh. So *that's* what the Crow meant. The figure places your gift on the nearest patch of soil and you watch with amazement as it swells up and returns to life. A bee immediately settles within the flower and starts to drink the nectar. The figure pushes you not-so gently towards the insect. You have no choice but to comply.

'You are here to learn how to leave.' The bee states with a thin, high-pitched whine, whilst wiping a drop of sugary liquid with its front legs. You nod.

'When you leave, you will face great dangers and none greater than Jezebeth, Demon of Falsehoods.'

'What about Carmichael? He's the one doing all the killing, isn't he?'

'He's definitely after all twelve powers and takes the organs to acquire them,' the bee agrees, 'but he couldn't do all this by himself. Think about it. The next victim is found; the world created to mirror theirs; the murderer is sent in to generate the fear needed to force the victim out of their own world and into this one.' You nod again, thinking about scared you were when you punched in that keycode to escape. The bee regards you with a sad expression. 'It takes more than just one mad man to do all that. He has help.'

You gulp and try to say something, but your throat is too dry. The bee continues, 'I shall open the exit for you, but you must find it. You've probably realised by now, that the organs are numbered and are the source of one particular power. For example, the intestines are the source of teleportation. There are symbols painted around the hospital and you should go to the symbol that has the same number that was with the intestines.'

If you know what this number is, multiply it by 12 and turn to that section. If you have no idea of what the bee is talking about, you have no choice but to don a long, waxed coat, a plague doctor mask and tend to the garden. It's not so bad. At least you're safe here.

191

You approach the corner tentatively. After all, the dogs do sound quite ferocious. If you are wearing a moonstone ring, turn to **335**. If not, turn to **44**.

192

Entering the quiet room, you switch the table lamp on and illuminate the cosy, safe space. There are soft cream walls with an inviting plump sofa and, over to the side, a single bed with…! You cry out, fear completely paralysing you and as much as you want to, you can't close your eyes. You can't help but stare…

There is a wizened form lying under the sheets and crouched on its chest is a blackened, malevolent form. It gazes at you with yellow eyes, then shifts on its haunches. Is it getting ready to attack? This thought frees your frozen muscles. If you want to try to talk to it, turn to **184**, but if you want to attack and strike first, turn to **267**.

193

Teetering on tiptoes, you stand on the edge of the chair arm and pull yourself up, inch by inch, until finally, you can see over the top.

And come face-to-face with the woman who's staring right back at you. You scream hysterically, let go and fall onto the floor, twisting your ankle.

Although you're hunched over, rubbing the swollen joint, you can still hear the shuffle of the *thing* coming around to you. With some trepidation, you turn to face her. She isn't pleasant. The face is purple and engorged with a thickened tongue protruding from her mouth. The neck looks elongated and dreadfully bruised.

'Not pretty, is it,' she states. 'We only had the short drop in 1612. It took eleven minutes for me to suffocate to death. Eleven minutes of dangling with all those jeering faces in front of me. I wished that I were a witch and I could curse them all for their cruelty and ignorance, but I wasn't. So I hung and I suffered. If only they would have rolled me down Pendle Hill in a barrel.'

If you think you know who this woman is, you should have a question for her. What will you ask?

Why does Carmichael want me?   Turn to **5**
Where is the Athame knife?   Turn to **77**

194

Success! The red-light changes to green and it unlocks. You have to really shove the heavy door to get it to open and then you step into a wide passageway. It's dark and gloomy and there are numerous doors with iron bars across the small observation windows. It looks like a prison, but you think this actually might have been the psychiatric ward. Of course, the intention then was never about making them better; it was about keeping them away from the 'normal' people. You walk a few steps, then reach a solid door on the left. You can hear a dripping sound inside the room and if you want to see what's causing that noise, turn to **107**. If you'd prefer to carry on along the passageway, turn to **368**.

195

The toilet is grubby and barely functional. The sort of place where you'd only go if you really had to and even then, you'd hover above the seat. You realise that, despite the passage of time, you don't need to use the toilet, which is probably because you've had nothing at all to drink. The basin is just in front of you. You could dip your head down and take a few glugs from the tap (turn to **138**) or just head straight back into the basement foyer (turn to **387**).

The pages are thick, well-thumbed and covered in fine, hand-written ink. You read headings such as 'Spells to enhance moods' and 'Scents that corrupt dreams' and realise that the Book of Shadows seems to be a collection of personal witchcraft knowledge. No wonder it wasn't happy about you holding it but maybe its true owner has gone forever. You skim through the chapters until you reach a beautifully painted chapter entitled 'The Power of Colours.'

> Blue: Tranquillity, dreams, water
> Red: Passion, courage, fire
> Orange: Energy, vitality, dominance
> Yellow: Mental clarity, stimulation, air
> Pink: Love, family, compassion
> Lilac: Psychic abilities and divination
> Indigo: Intuition, occult wisdom, healing
> Green: Fertility, growth, nature
> Brown Animals, home, earth
> White: Purifies, peace, justice
> Black: Removes negativity and banishes evil
> Silver: The Goddess, Moon, balance
> Gold: Wealth, power, Sun

You decide that this book may be useful so place it carefully in your bag. Make a note of this section number, so you can refresh your knowledge of colours if you need to in the future

Now turn to **147**, so you can finally leave the lecture theatre.

197

You can either go straight on towards the heavy steel door (turn to **322**) or head right (turn to **136**).

198

Being on the floor, you are disadvantaged, and he knows it. He smirks, then bolts forward. You try to leap away, but he punches you hard in the chest. It takes your breath and for a second you are stunned. And confused. Why is he just waiting? You look down and see the hilt of the knife protruding from between your ribs. Oh, it wasn't a punch then. Almost transfixed, you watch the rhythmical movement of the handle, realising that it's moving with each beat of your heart, which can only mean one thing. The motion slows as your sliced heart leaks blood with each beat. Just before you die, you hear him hiss, 'About time. My mistress will be glad to see the back of you.'

199

You feel safe enough on this linking corridor. It has no rooms or doors, so nothing can jump out at you but just before you get too complacent, your foot skids and you almost fall. You look at the floor and in the dim light, can see that it's not just a single smear of blood. It's everywhere! Thick droplets and footprints cover the floor — as if someone drenched in it had been searching the area...

With your pulse racing, you pick up the pace and reach the junction where a left turn will take you back in the direction of the operating theatres (turn to **226**) and a right turn would normally take you to the medical wards, but it seems to be blocked off with some strange barrier now (turn to **202**). Where do you decide to go?

200

You slide the largest bottle of laudanum to one side and press your fingertips against the panel behind it. The entire wall of shelving swings round on a pivot with a protesting groan. Beyond, and lit with flickering gas lamps, is a mahogany-lined corridor. You enter and walk to the door at the far end. It is covered with intricate carvings and inscribed in the middle are the following two lines:

ZM ZGIRFN LI ZM RMUVXGRLM

TZRM ZXXVHH GSILFTS GSV ULFIGS HVXGRLM

If you don't know how to decipher the code, you can rattle the handle a few times until you realise that you're just not going to get into Jezebeth's secret room. You did well to get this far but it simply wasn't good enough to end this nightmarish nightshift.

201

Putting the sickly-yellow colour behind you, you wonder what to do now. You could investigate the bathroom if you haven't done so already (turn to **217**) or else you can head to the ward exit (turn to **274**).

You edge towards the bizarre barrier, feeling revulsion spread inside you. Is that...? You peer closer and confirm your worst fears. It's skin; many peoples' skins sutured together and stretched across the entire width of the corridor and from floor to ceiling. You can see belly buttons, freckles and tattoos, and in the top right-hand corner is a symbol. You wrack your memory and finally remember — it's a triqueta. A shape made up of 3 overlapping circles. What was going on? What did it mean?

If you want to examine the skin more closely, turn to **350**, but if you'd prefer to tear the skin to get to the other side, turn to **209**.

You step out of the blackness and into a thin, cold, concrete corridor. The fluorescent bulbs are weak and flickering, but it's enough light for you to see the injuries all over your body. Not just bruises — although there are plenty of those — but deep cuts. They were after your blood! They were feeding on you! You feel dizzy and slump to the floor, wondering just how much blood they drained. You close your eyes telling yourself that you just need a short nap to boost your energy and then you'll be OK but deep down, you know the truth. A combination of shock and cold means that you won't wake up from this. It's a pitiful end but look on the bright side — it could have been much worse.

204

You continue walking along the passageway, until you start to smell flowers. Lots of flowers! Now that might happen on the wards but not in x-ray, so where is the scent coming from? There's some chairs and newspapers in a small waiting area. That just smells musty, but if you want to take a break there, turn to **341**. To your right is a closed door with a red bulb above it. The light is switched on, meaning 'Danger! X-rays in operation', so if you'd like to see who is taking x-rays, turn to **75**. If neither of those options appeal, you can simply walk straight ahead and exit the department (turn to **208**).

205

After a few steps in this direction, you have a choice to make. Where should you go now?

Left	Turn to **302**
Right	Turn to **137**

206

There are no doors and no other turn-offs, so you have no option but to head up the staircase. The stone floor of the corridor gives way to a burgundy carpet that covers the stair treads like a draped tongue. It's a steep climb and at the top, the corridor simply carries straight on. It's lit by skylights which allow the bright sunshine to come streaming down. You walk along, passing by two open doors. Each room looks the same — a narrow bed, chest of drawers, wardrobe, sink and desk. It looks dated but familiar. This must have been the old nurses' residence. The third door is closed, but before you open it to have a look, you pause. Something has caught your eye. Strangely shaped shadows on the carpet that are definitely not being cast by the skylights above. If you want to go ahead and examine these shapes closer, turn to **336**, but if you think you should check out what's behind the closed door, turn to **359**.

207

Once you're out of the stairwell, you feel a huge sense of relief but at the same time, really stupid. Was that just a total over-reaction? You shake your head, trying to get a grip. You can't afford to lose it now. There's enough going on without you dissolving into a puddle of hysteria. Eventually, you take a deep breath in and head into the Recovery area (turn to **117**).

208

You open the door and step into the darkest corridor you've ever seen. You get your pen torch out, but its weak light barely penetrates this inky blackness before the batteries die. You give a nervous swallow and start having second thoughts about this route but decide to grit your teeth and go forward. The door closes behind you and the darkness is now complete. You hold your hand in front of your eyes but can see absolutely nothing. Feeling the panic rise quickly, you reach out to the wall — anything tangible to reassure yourself, but what you feel is anything but reassuring. It is rough, bone-chillingly cold and seems to be covered with moss or mould. You can't stop your imagination from conjuring up images of caves. Is that where you are? You've only taken a few steps so if you've changed your mind and would rather head back into the x-ray department, turn to **43**. If you're thinking that you've come this far, you'll see it through, turn to **352**.

209

You find the closest sections that are sutured together and wiggle your fingers through. It feels a bit disgusting, but you've handled worse things in your job, so you persevere until both hands are through. You then start pulling them apart and... success! The sutures begin to pop open. You can see through the gap and it looks normal. You can even see people in the distance. Normal people doing normal things. In your desperation to reach them, you push your arms further through the skin edges, but it's feeling strange now.

You look down and see a tight puckering of your own skin where it's touching the barrier and realise that the two skins are entwining. You're becoming a part of it!

In a mad panic, you pull back without thinking and cry out as pieces of your own skin are stripped off. Before your very eyes, you watch as it fills the gap you'd made. There's no way you're getting through there, so wincing, you turn your back on the barrier and think about where to go next. Do you want to head straight on (turn to **226**) or go left (turn to **125**)?

210

Now you can decide to go either straight ahead (turn to **35**) or left and head back to the crossroads (turn to **136**).

211

At first, you think the door is locked but there's a slight give, and with a little more tugging you pull it open. A gust of cold air takes your breath away and you can see, courtesy of some flickering fluorescent lights in the distance, that this door leads to a straight, thin, windowless, concrete passageway that, if your eyes don't deceive you, is sloping gradually down. You shiver in your scrubs and wonder if this is the best move. Do you decide to step into this corridor and see where it takes you to (turn to **310**) or head back to the ivy-covered corridor (turn to **7**)?

212

You push open the door to the ward and enter, but before you can take another step, a hand grabs you by the throat and slams you off your feet, back against the door. You feel something crack in your spine — a momentous pain followed by a weird nothingness. Your legs dangle uselessly, as the man grabs you underneath the armpits and hoists you over his shoulder. You can smell the blood soaked into his clothing. Nancy's blood.

'Did you really think that you could get away from me by guessing? Nobody guesses here. You either know or you die. My Master is going to be very happy to get the twelfth one. The *last* one! Very happy indeed.' He carries you off and as your head bangs repeatedly against his back with every step, you wonder: Which body part is going to be harvested?

213

You put the last key into its lock and hold your breath. Turn to **15**.

214

Without giving yourself a chance to change your mind, you set off running as quick as you can. You skid slightly as you take the corner, and although you see it in time, you can't stop your forward momentum. You fall into the deep pit in the middle of the passageway. Turn to **73**.

You try to push the door open, but it's stuck at the bottom. You heave with all your strength, hearing it scrape against the floor and when the gap is big enough, you attempt to squeeze through. Just as you're wedged in the space, having serious doubts about the wisdom of this manoeuvre, you see a shadow shift ahead of you. You gasp and try to pull back, but your scrubs get caught. A tall figure steps from behind the door and stands in front of you. For a second, you both stare at each other. It's wearing a long, waxed coat, a beaked plague doctor mask and is holding a kidney in the right hand. It's quite a sight and for a few seconds, you're too dumbstruck to be frightened.

'What do you want? I'm busy,' it barks at you, the voice muffled by the beak.

'I want to get out of here,' you eventually stutter. It sighs impatiently then,

'Well?' Its left hand is outstretched waiting for you to put something in it. 'I haven't got all day. This kidney won't transplant itself!'

You have a look of confusion on your face as you think about the items stuffed in your pockets. What does it want? But before you can come to any decision, it pushes you firmly in the chest away from the door and then forces it shut again. You have no choice now but to carry on along the corridor (turn to **2**).

216

If you wish to head right towards a closed door, turn to **374**. Alternatively, you could go left and see where this other passageway leads to (turn to **134**) but if you'd prefer to go straight on, where the corridor leads to a staircase, turn to **206**.

217

You open the door and for a second, think that there's nothing here. Just an old tin bath and a wooden bucket. Something makes you step a little further though, and then you see the water, which is filling the bath and the naked old woman lying under the surface. Her eyes and her mouth are gaping open and when you touch the water, you recoil at how cold it is. Suddenly, the old woman locks her eyes on you and sits up. The icy water splashes up and her frozen hand grips your arm like a clamp.

'Did you think I'd drowned?' she asks, 'Did you?' You nod frantically, still trying to prise her fingers off your arm.

'How can I drown if I have no lungs?' She says almost triumphantly, as if she'd won some bet or game. With that, she lets go of you and slumps against the back of the tub, gazing at you with bored eyes. You're getting used to this now, so you ask the obvious question.

'Did Carmichael take your lungs?' The old woman snorts at the name and nods.

'What power did he get from them?' You continue, curious now rather than scared.

'I had the power of levitation and he called me number 9. People started making up stories about witches flying around on broomsticks but that was just nonsense. Can you imagine trying to balance on a broomstick? Of course not! It's too thin for a start. Ridiculous. But we can levitate, and I suppose some careless old witch let herself be seen and that's where the tales came from. Next thing you know, we're fornicating with Satan and being burnt. Or hanged. Or drowned.' With the final word, she slaps both hands against the water's surface in frustration.

'I am trying to stop all this,' you tell her, 'but is there anything I can do now to help you?' Although she shakes her head sulkily, she pats your arm for this kindness.

'Just remember that if you're concocting any spells or potions, the cup or container you mix everything in is just as important as the ingredients themselves. It's usually specific to the spell but as a rule of thumb, you can't go wrong with silver.' With that, she slips back under the water to resume her icy vigil.

You leave the bathroom and can go to the day room if you haven't been there already (turn to **112**) or head back out of the ward (turn to **274**).

218

You reach out with a trembling hand, hoping that someone is there to help you. The buzzer gives out a piercing, off-key whine which abruptly dies. And then you hear it. Whispering. There are voices all around you.

'Someone's here. Someone's here. Now the fun starts. How long will they last? Are they coming here?' You give a muted cry, then bolt back down the corridor. Turn to **311**.

219

Fittingly, the furnace room is red. A glossy, cochineal red that makes your blood start pumping hot and fast, just by being there. There is no actual heat — the furnaces are cold. There are two at one end of the room and both have their doors open. You can see the piles of grey ash inside and wonder about the amputated limbs and who knows what that have been burnt down here. There's seems to be nothing more in the room but, while you're here, you could investigate whether there's anything left in the furnaces. If not, you can always leave. What will you do?

Look inside the left furnace	Turn to **38**
Look inside the right furnace	Turn to **103**
Leave the red room	Turn to **347**

220

You need to finish your spell before the demon comes up with something new. You pick up your concoction from the counter and prepare to add the final ingredient — the dying breath. If you know how to do this, you should have received the code words. Turn the words into a number by using the code: A=1, B=2, C=3 ….. Z=26. Add *this* number to the current section and then turn to the section with that new, bigger number. If you don't know the words, you cannot finish the spell and you can rest assured that Jezebeth still has plenty of tricks up her sleeve. Your nightshift has finally ended.

221

Holding the candle high in the air and panicking as the noise from above becomes more agitated, you whisper the name Hestia. Nothing happens. You say it again, a little louder but not too loud, just in case… And suddenly, a tiny flickering flame appears on the wick. It takes hold, becoming bigger and stronger and casting a supernaturally bright light around the cave. You look up and your jaw drops as you see the row upon row of large birds hanging upside down from the roof of the cave. They have grey feathers and large, dangerous beaks, which seem to be coated in blood. Oh great, you think, watching them twitch wings and peck each other. It appears as though they're about to launch themselves into the air for an attack and let's face it — that doesn't look good for you. However, the agitation settles and although a few of them give their neighbour an irritated jab, most of them tuck their heads under their wings and go to sleep. You realise that there is a scent coming from the candle and give a few sniffs. It's sandalwood. The aroma rises up, swirling around you, then drifting amongst the raptors. It's like ether for birds and you take the opportunity to speed up and get away from them. With the bright flame, you can see the exit ahead and make your way quickly to it. Turn to **389**.

222

You step off the staircase into a low layer of green mist and despite this incongruous fog, it's clear that you're in the laboratories. Of course, you pass by them every day on your way to the theatres — there's just never been a reason to go inside them. All around you are typical lab workbenches but instead of high-tech equipment, there's just row upon row of specimen jars. You scrutinise one that is half-filled with a thick black viscous fluid. It looks like crude oil but protruding from the surface, are thick black spider's legs. You withdraw in disgust. It seems like most of the exhibits are animals — mice foetuses, a dissected spinal cord only 6 centimetres long, a tongue… Hang on a minute! You pick up the glass jar, rotating it slowly, feeling the nausea build up. It has only one label stuck to it, which says '3' and the tongue looks distinctly human!

Abruptly, you hear a thin scratching sound from behind, so you turn and see words being gouged into the wall tiles.

free me

Free me? Free who, you wonder. The tongue? If you decide to reach into the jar to carefully extract the body part, turn to **13**. If you think that dropping the jar onto the floor is a safer option, turn to **33**.

223

You walk down the central corridor past many single bedrooms. It makes sense — if you're investigating sleep, it helps if people can actually sleep and, let's face it, some of these patients are *loud* snorers. It's quiet now though as you reach a junction and have to choose whether to carry on straight ahead (turn to **155**) or turn left (turn to **247**). Just as you're stood there in a state of indecision, you notice a lump in the bed in the room nearest to you. It looks like legs, which means you now have a third option and if you want to enter the bedroom, turn to **297**.

224

Keeping your back pressed tightly against the wall, you inch your way around the side of the pit. With each step, you envisage slipping and hurtling into the depths, but finally, you make it safely to the other side. Breathing a deep sigh of relief, you open the doors and enter the Children's Ward (turn to **281**).

225

You open the fridge door. There is a small, shrouded corpse but you're sure that the exit must be here. You have no choice but to climb in. The door slams shut behind you and the darkness is total. You feel your way forward, apologising to the thin, shrivelled body, but suddenly, bony arms encircle your waist holding you close in a macabre embrace. You wriggle with mounting disgust, but it isn't letting go of you. With the exertion and panic, you start to sweat and only then realise that the temperature is dropping even more. It will take hours before the hypothermia finally kills you, but at least you have company.

226

You're striding quickly down this familiar passageway, when suddenly, you're plunged into a pitch-black nightmare. The emergency lighting has either failed or been switched off! You stand there, frozen yet hyperventilating and the only noise is a dull, repetitive thudding coming from the right. Eventually, there is an electric hum and the lights flicker back on. You had stopped between two rooms. Would you like to go into the neuro-surgical unit on your right (turn to **268**), the prayer room on your left (turn to **11**) or just carry on along the passageway (turn to **338**)?

227

There is no lock on this door, so you exit the psychiatric ward without any bother and climb the short staircase. At the top, you reach a wide passageway running left to right. The signpost on the wall opposite tells you that the Geriatrics ward is to the left (turn to **25**) and the Sleep Disorders Laboratory is to the right (turn to **382**). Where do you want to go now?

228

You step out onto the patio area of a walled garden. Despite the dogs, it is a peaceful place with trees moving gently in a breeze, casting dappled shadows onto the paving stones. The barking seems to be coming from around the corner, and if you want to face the hounds, turn to **191**.

If not, there is a bubbling fountain and a campfire nearby, so if you have a small cauldron, you could boil some water. If this sounds tempting, turn to **293**.

229

You place the silver chalice on the table and take a deep breath. This is really happening. If you can do this right, you just might make it back. You feel a little trickle of sweat weave down your temple, then you pull the photo out of the bag. You have no idea how the image of you ended up in the mortuary, but it must mean something. You are the executioner, after all, so with a decisive move, you crumple up the photo and stuff it into the chalice. Next, you're going to mix it with some blood. If you have a recipe of this spell, you should know where to take the blood from; if not, you'll just have to guess and keep your fingers crossed. Which organ do you squeeze until the blood drips into the chalice?

| The heart | Turn to **320** |
| The uterus | Turn to **165** |

230

You yank the handle down and pull the door open. You slide through the gap then desperately turn to close it. The shadow looms nearer. The door closes but slowly, oh, so slowly. You feel a scream ripping at the side of your throat. Come on! And then it clicks, just as the handle rattles. Your heart stops for a second but you hear a curse and a fist slammed on the door. You slump down the walls, legs too weak to hold you up but blood thudding through your ears. Gradually, you start to breathe again and then you look around.

You're in a corridor that you know well but not like this. The dim night-time light can't disguise how run-down and abandoned it is. This isn't normal. You can see patches of damp and spores all over the walls. The paint is peeling off and a thick layer of grime lies underneath your fingers. You get up, using the wall as leverage, but snatch your hand away as a spider runs over it. What's going on?

You stand with your back to the door you've just escaped through. The corridor leading to the Intensive Care Unit is to the left and if you decide to head there, turn to **127**. However, if you go straight ahead, you'll reach the main hospital thoroughfare, and if you think that's a better option, turn to **276**.

231

You put the last key into its lock and hold your breath. Turn to **183**.

232

The jet-black smoke spirals up and around the room and both you and Jezebeth watch it in stunned silence for what seems like an eternity. You're starting to wonder what went wrong when a high-pitched whining fills the room. Jezebeth's face is contorting, the jaws opening, and she brings her claws up to scrape at the dried strands of muscle in her face. You back away, still holding the smoking chalice tight to your chest and suddenly, the demon twists down. You gasp in shock as Jezebeth starts to ingest her own tail. Coiled around on herself, she keeps feeding and feeding, her mouth stretching wider and wider with each swallow. You can only stare as the demon gradually eats herself out of existence and with the final morsel, the flame is extinguished. Turn to **400**.

233

You grab the laboratory door handle and pull, but it's locked. You're trapped. Instantly, you panic and look around for something to smash through the door with. But then you notice a small petri dish that's glowing with a soft pink luminescence. You go over to it, mesmerised by the colour and see that it's labelled 'Crushed sea eagle talons'. If you wish to take it, put it in your pocket. You head back to the door, a little calmer now, and see that a key is already in the lock. Berating yourself for that hysteria, you open the door and set off down a small corridor. You pass by other laboratories and offices, and head directly for the main ground floor thoroughfare. Turn to **140**.

You emerge from the mirror into a room that looks nothing like the reflection. It's more like a gentleman's study in a stately home, with Chesterfield winged armchairs, books strewn everywhere and the unpleasant smell of stale whisky and cigars. Is this Carmichael's hide-out?

As interesting as that may be, you came here for the box, so you reach down for it but feel a burning pain between your shoulder blades. It's like someone is drawing a hot knife round and round, over your skin. You pull up your top and peer into the mirror you've just walked through. It's as though you've been branded — a blackened, charred spiral is nestled in the middle of your back. You poke the flesh tentatively and wince. You're not sure what's going on here, so it's probably best to leave as soon as you can, but you do want to have a quick look around this mirror-room first. It has so many things that are not there in the real world. If you can call the other side 'real'…

If you want to examine the microscope standing on the desk, turn to **173**, but if you'd rather inspect the crystal decanter on the sideboard, turn to **295**.

You feel confident that you're right — after all, you just had to double the previous number then add 1. You look up expectantly and are instantly rewarded with a huge smile.

'Well done!' she cries, clapping her hands together. 'Now, listen carefully. You will not survive without this knowledge. A most powerful weapon is the dying breath. You must collect it in readiness.' There is a long pause. You stare disbelieving at her — seriously? Collect a dying breath? You ask, 'How?' and the washerwoman frowns, looking as if she's never met someone as dumb as you in her whole life.

'You breathe it in. Obviously.'

'And then hold my breath? For how long?' You say in frustration. She shakes her head at you.

'No. It'll come out when the time is right. Obviously.'

For the next few seconds, you simply stare at each other, but eventually, you decide to just go with the flow. After everything that's happened so far, it's probably for the best!

'Thank you for the advice,' you say graciously, and the washerwoman smiles again, then points to the far end of the room.

'Off you go now. I've got work to do. I can't spend all day talking to you.' And with that, you are dismissed. Turn to **79**.

236

Eventually, you reach a door — the exit! If you want to leave the prison-like ward, turn to **227**, however, there is a closed door to your left and you can hear a strange noise coming from within. If you want to see what's happening in there, turn to **284**.

237

You soon arrive at a set of doors. The sign welcomes you to the Geranium Unit with a simple picture of a five-petalled purple flower. It's pretty but it doesn't tell you what to expect inside. If you decide to enter anyway, turn to **258**, but if you don't want to risk venturing into the unknown, turn around and head back in the opposite direction (turn to **304**).

238

Jezebeth looks you up and down, but what is she searching for? Eventually, she gives a whip-crack flick of the tail and glares furiously at you. Like a thunderbolt, you realise what's happening She's trying to take control of you but can't. Now, you feel emboldened. It's time to strike back! Turn to **220**.

You peek over the counter of the Information Desk to see if there's anything useful there. Ivy is growing over and around the desktop, but you can see there is a scroll within the tendrils. You reach down and unravel it, trying not to breathe in the musty smell that emanates from the parchment and read:

> When you need the Athame knife
> Seek the counsel of Pendle's wife

That might be useful, you think, so you roll it back up and tuck it into your sock. Turn to **55**.

You crouch down by Nathanael's chair, almost asphyxiated by the stench of ammonia. Poor man, you think, does this nurse do nothing for them?

'Excuse me, sir, can you tell me anything?'
Nathanael points a shaking finger at the far wall. You turn to look but it's just yellow. You're not sure what it means and when you turn back, his head has sagged against his chest. You stand up, ready to go, but then he mutters, 'It's a type of tree'. You wait but those words of wisdom are the only thing he says.
You leave the day room (turn to **315**).

You pluck your trusty biro out of the scrubs pocket and scribble in the missing letters L and B. As you turn the page an advert catches your eye. It's a Victorian man complete with stovepipe hat and extravagant moustache, but his entire body is a carrot. Apparently, this is meant to entice you to buy seeds. You raise your eyebrows at how bizarre it is. You're just about to put the newspaper down when the carrot-man moves. He puts his carrot-arms on his hips and shouts, 'Are you deaf?'

You actually look around, for a second wondering who he's talking to, but then realise that, of course, he's shouting at you. You sigh and reply, 'No, I can hear you. It's nice to meet you.'

'Quite. Now then, well done for completing the puzzle. It wasn't difficult but that's not the point. There are many strange things going on here.'

Says the talking carrot-man, you think wryly, but still manage to nod encouragingly. He continues, 'And if you need to find out certain pieces of information — how to decipher codes, for example — just submerge yourself underwater.' There's a pregnant pause, while you take in this nugget.

'I have to drown myself?'

'Good Heavens, have you lost all your senses? Can you not understand basic English? I said submerge, not drown. And your entire body. Don't think that sticking your head underneath will suffice because it won't. Now, have you finally understood?' You nod and the newspaper instantly becomes engulfed in a golden flame. You gasp, leaping onto your feet and throwing the burning mass away. All that remains are the black wisps of paper, which float slowly down like snowflakes. You can now leave the department either by the way you entered (turn to **17**) or the opposite exit (turn to **208**), or if you haven't yet tried the door with the red warning light and would like to do so now, turn to **75**.

242

Your heart sinks as you walk down the thoroughfare. You were hoping that it would look normal; that you'd finally woken up from a nightmare but no. If anything, it looks even worse. Ceiling tiles are hanging down from the twisted metal struts and there are deep, long gouges in the few vestiges of plaster on the walls. If you didn't know better, you'd say that it was claw marks, but it couldn't be, could it? You take a deep breath and approach the corner. You can either follow the corridor around to the left (turn to **61**) or investigate the nearby Vascular ward (turn to **177**).

243

The scabbed-over puncture marks throb and a watery liquid begins to ooze out, trickling down your fingers. Are you carrying a braided snake-skin bracelet?

Yes   Turn to **277**
No   Turn to **139**

244

You cross to the right side of the foyer and stare up at the chiselled face. It regards you with an imperious expression and the engraving on the plinth tells you that this is a statue of Matthew Hopkins. You feel an urge to touch the smooth marble cheek, but what do you actually do next? Examine the statue closer (turn to **269**); go over to the mirror (turn to **386**) or head for the double doors (turn to **41**).

245

It's a narrow passageway — you can touch both walls if you stretch your arms out wide — and it's pitch-black. You seem to have walked for ages, when you think that either your eyes are finally getting used to the dark or it is actually getting lighter. A few steps further and you're certain. It is definitely brighter and now you can see your surroundings. Except... It looks like you're in an attic! How can that be? You started out in the basement. You haven't climbed any stairs and the passageway wasn't sloping but here you are. Eaves on either side and joists under your feet. You walk on cautiously, hearing your footsteps creak loudly. That's a worry — anyone walking on the floor below will be able to hear that! You're relieved when you reach the end of the attic and see the staircase. You might as well continue, even though you have absolutely no idea where you are now. Down and down you go, into the dark again until finally you reach a door. You open it and step through. Well, you think, this looks familiar. Turn to **99**.

246

This is where you work, and you know that this poor woman's liver wasn't ripped out by hand. Something sharp was used and that could be a perfect weapon. You rummage through the cupboards and assemble a scalpel. It's not much, but it's better than nothing. You put the knife carefully in your pocket, then head for the scrub up area where the exit door is. Turn to **306**.

247

Before long, you exit the Sleep Laboratory and continue down the corridor. Finally, you go around a corner and arrive at a grand foyer. Turn to **108**.

248

The door softly closes behind you and you're back in the corridor. You could turn right, which takes you out of the x-ray department, although to where, you have no idea. The chairs are still there, so if you haven't done so already and you want to take a break, now's your chance. The only other option is to go left, back from where you came from. What will you do now?

Go right	Turn to **208**
Take a break	Turn to **341**
Go left	Turn to **17**

Before you even see it, you just know that Jezebeth is here. The demon stands before you, swaying slightly from side to side on a thick serpent body. The scales are a dull taupe colour but with shimmering edges of amber. The torso and head are that of a skeleton, albeit one with dried and leathery flesh tightly gripping the bones underneath. Her eyes are huge black holes and the jaw contains fiercely sharp snake fangs. A voice fills your head, although you don't see Jezebeth mouthing any words. You are practically numb with fear, listening to the confident and condescending laugh as the demon appraises you. There are a few seconds in which you could do something to escape or fight, but you can't. You don't have everything you need to destroy her. You've blown your chance.

Jezebeth realises this and smiles, her mouth widening and stretching until eventually, her jaw unhinges and she sinks her fangs around your skull. You are frozen and can do nothing now but wait while she ingests you whole, one swallow at a time.

You ask your question and chew nervously on your bottom lip as the Crow contemplates it.

'Good. Good. Stay focused and you just might make it through. Yes. Get out. Well, for that all you need to know is that when you've left, you will be right, if you turn left then you turn right. All the Bs and tell the bees. Give the flower, the beak to please.' It snaps its head in your direction, gives a sharp nod, then does a strange flapping and jumping walk towards the dark corner of the room and promptly disappears.

You sit there for a while, staring open-mouthed but finally, you realise that the Crow isn't coming back. That was it. That was your help to get out of here. You leave the room and where do you go now?

| Left | Turn to **130** |
| Right | Turn to **205** |

You drink the chamomile tea and feel soothed by both the warmth and the herbs. Once you've finished, you realise that the dogs have stopped barking. There seems to be nothing else here in the garden, so you head back inside and continue along the corridor. Turn to **301**.

After all that you've seen, you are expecting the worst and you're right. You tug back the curtain and face the ripe corpse on the bed. The legs are up in stirrups, but the abdomen has been cut open too. It is an abomination of something that is meant to be a happy event. She is grey and mottled and the cavity is undulating with an endless parade of flies. Despite the mass of feasting insects, it looks suspiciously empty. You have no idea what happened to the baby after it was born, but you're sure that the uterus was taken too and you know *all* about that now. Her eyes are cloudy and her mouth gapes open, but you still take her cold hand in yours and say, 'Can you help me?' There is a long pause but finally, she slowly blinks and looks at you.

'I am Gretl, but for so long I have been number 10. I lost three things on that fateful day. I wish I could reclaim my child, womb and power as I reclaim my name, but that will never be.' A tear rolls down her sunken cheek and you feel at a loss. What can you say?

'What power did your womb give?'   Turn to **349**
'Can I help you to find your baby?'   Turn to **100**

You step off the ladder and take a good look around. There is a body on the post-mortem table, but it's shrouded with a white sheet. Otherwise, everything is as quiet as the grave. Do you examine the body on the table (turn to **319**) or head for the door (turn to **157**)?

You turn around, ready to face whatever is there. A stocky, middle-aged man with dark sideburns and a moustache is stood between the operating table and a blackboard. Although you think you know who this is, you see 'Carmichael Jezebeth' scrawled on the board in chalk. For a few seconds, you stare at each other but then surprisingly, he smiles.

'My final witch,' he claims warmly. 'I have waited so long for you and your power.'

'I'm not a witch,' you stutter, 'I'm a nurse. I have no power. I just want to go home.' Your words have no effect though — he simply shakes his head indulgently.

'Exactly. My nurse witch with her healing hands. Soon to be *my* hands.'

The blood drains from your head as you realise what he's saying, but a burst of adrenalin courses through you. *Not bloody likely!* you think, before shouting, 'There's no way you're cutting my hands off!'

You turn to run and go straight into the other man, the murderer. He grips you instantly in a headlock, your face pressing into the blood-soaked shirt he's still wearing, and although you try to fight him off, he's just too strong. With your air running out, you vaguely feel your arms being straightened, then a searing shock of pain. Before you die, you hear him thank you for your gift and tell you that you are number 0.

255

As strange as it sounds, you're actually glad to be back in the black cave-like corridor. Still, it takes a while to get used to the absence of the green light, but you're making good progress when your way is blocked by solid stone. Keeping an almost constant contact with the wall, you follow the path around to the right and slowly walk forward. Turn to **373**.

256

You slosh along the corridor and pass by a stairwell, but when you cautiously try to open the door, surprisingly, it is locked. That means, your options are now limited. You can follow the corridor around to the right as it leads to the rest of the hospital (turn to **135**) or go straight ahead through the double doors into the main entrance foyer (turn to **343**).

257

You turn sideways and squeeze through the narrow space into the strangest yet cosiest room. As far as you can see, the walls and the ceiling are draped with a grey woollen tapestry. The interwoven fibres are of varying shades, from a mossy-stone to Payne's grey giving an undulating, ever-shifting impression. Under your feet lies a gun-metal coloured carpet, which you sink into as you look around. Your breath quickens when you notice the three figures occupying three corners of the room.

If you want to immediately leave this room and head back to the junction, turn to **197** but if you decide to speak to these silent strangers, turn to **69**.

258

You enter the unit then stop, stunned by the thousands upon thousands of pieces of paper plastered onto the walls, ceiling and doors. All the windows have been papered over, blocking the light out, and on all these pages are the scribblings of millions of words. You step closer to read it, but you can't understand the language; come to think of it, you don't even recognise the alphabet. Sometimes, out of the corner of your eye, you see the odd sentence part: 'when fungi migrate', 'sycophantic leanings' and 'appears wholly consumed yet' but when you turn to examine it, the words metamorphose back into a foreign tongue. The air is musty, dusty and feels oppressive, but at the far end of the corridor, you see an abandoned, empty crib. This has to be the maternity unit then, and your suspicion is proved correct when you find a hidden door nearby with the sign: Delivery Room. If you want to enter the room, turn to **372**. If not, you should carry on along the corridor (turn to **119**).

259

With your face furrowed in concentration, you grope around, trying to reach all corners. Suddenly, you feel a tugging then a sharp pain, and you yank your hand out. Your finger is bleeding from two incisor-shaped wounds — you've been bitten and by a rat if you're not mistaken! With thoughts of rabies whirling round your head, you curse your curiosity and find a tissue to mop the blood up. Once it's started to clot, you pick up the roll of paper. Turn to **367**.

260

The swamp soon dries up and becomes a normal floor again. The thoroughfare widens to become a seating area for those who need to catch their breath. Except... Those people are not just resting. You squint at the limp forms slumped on the chairs. Their skin looks putrid — bloated with a hint of green and dark threads spreading out all over the surface.

If you want to pass quickly through to the other side, where the corridor continues, turn to **377**. If you want to turn around and return to the swamp, turn to **42**.

261

Suddenly, your hands hit a wall straight ahead. You follow its contours and realise that you are in a corner with no going left, so — right it is! Despite everything, you're feeling proud of your progress. Turn to **373**.

It's a huge, cavernous room, reminiscent of Victorian mills. When all the dryers were working, it must have been a cacophony, but now, there is just an echoing stillness. The sun is streaming in through the windows, which is nice but isn't it supposed to be night-time?

Suddenly, one of the dryers opens up and scrambling out from the depths comes a barrel of a woman. Her clothing is that of a typical Victorian servant, but she has a face like a toad. She nods curtly at you, then brushes down her pinafore. When satisfied, she gives a huff and plants her hands on her hips.

'Which number are you?' she asks with the husky voice of a lifelong smoker. You shrug, shaking your head.

'Well, you've still got all your bits, I see, so you're doing better than most.' She seems to be harmless, so you ask her,

'Do you know where I go now?'

She laughs like a drain at this, rocking back and forth, slapping her hands on her thighs with each forward movement until the laughing turns into coughing. With an alarmingly ruddy face, she eventually says, 'No', takes a drink of water from a nearby tap then continues. 'Not me, dearie, but I do know the numbers are important. Take the number 3, for example. In pagan lore, 3 is communication, and where did you find it?'

You wrack your brain — so much has happened in such a short time — but before you can answer, she carries on. 'Number 3 was the poor witch who had her tongue ripped out. Oh yes, mark my words, the numbers are vital if you intend to survive.'

'Is there anything else you can tell me?'

'Yes, but only if you answer my riddle.'

If you want to play her game, turn to **318**. If you decide to start walking to the far end of the room, turn to **79**.

263

You look tentatively at the bottles — ether and chloroform — and are hoping that none of the vapours are seeping out when a thought occurs to you. Could Jezebeth's secret room be close by? Just as you consider the possibility, the shelves seem to lurch and slide before your eyes. Your attempt to grab onto something to prevent the fall is futile and by the time you hit the floor, you are already deeply unconscious. You will never know what happened then or how you ended up back at the start, but maybe next time, you won't make the same mistakes. Turn to **1**.

264

You start examining the boxes of disposable face masks. When you pick up the third box and shake it, you can feel a weight shift inside. You tip it upside down onto the nearest bed and a puffin's beak falls out. You're not exactly happy about picking it up, but something so incongruous *has* to mean something. You put it into your pocket for safe-keeping and head for the exit. Turn to **8**.

265

You nervously open the door and peer in. It seems like a bright and clean room, but is it safe? Did you make the right choice? You take a step forward and the door slams behind you — there's no going back. It looks like a traditional Victorian ward with a large desk in the middle of the room, separating the opposing rows of beds. Everything is in place and even the sheets have hospital corners. In fact, the only thing missing is the patients and nurses. You decide to explore the ward and can see signs for the bathroom and the patients' day room. Where will you go?

To the bathroom	Turn to **337**
To the day room	Turn to **58**

266

Being on the floor, you are disadvantaged, and he knows it. He smirks, then bolts forward. You try to leap away, but he punches you hard in the chest. It takes your breath and for a second you are stunned. And confused. Why is he just waiting? You look down and see the hilt of the knife protruding from between your ribs. Oh, not a punch then. Almost transfixed, you watch the rhythmical movement of the handle, realising that it's moving with each beat of your heart, which can only mean one thing. The motion slows as your sliced heart leaks blood with each beat. Just before you die, you hear him hiss, 'About time. My mistress will be glad to see the back of you.'

There is a hardback novel on the nearby bookcase, which you grab and hurl at the thing. In a comedy of errors though, it goes in completely the wrong direction, hits the lamp, which shatters the bulb and plunges the room back into darkness. You hold your breath in shock — what have you done? You can hear the thing shuffling around and then it says in a low, gravelly voice, 'Thank goodness for that. The light was blinding me!' You hear it yawn extravagantly and despite the dark, you don't feel half so scared now, so you ask, 'What are you? Some sort of demon? A succubus?'

It makes a snorting noise that sounds like disapproval.

'The thing that you say takes souls while you sleep? Always maligned, always misunderstood...' it trails off mournfully. You're actually feeling sorry for it now, so you ask, 'What *do* you do then?'

'Humans will always have bad dreams. It's in your nature. We take them *away* from you. We *stop* your suffering. Granted, they are quite tasty too; the more frightening the dream, the more delicious it is, but that's not the point!'

You're not too sure what to say to this, but in the end, you opt for a polite 'thank you'. It seems to be the safest option. The succubus sounds surprised but grateful.

'You're welcome. We call ourselves 'mare' and if you see a portrait of one of us, say the name and they will give good advice. We, too, are tired of being trapped here.' You repeat the name 'mare', say thank you again, then turn to leave the quiet room. As you slip out, the light from the hallway seeps in and you see the thing wrapping its long, spidery limbs around each other. Before you close the door, it murmurs, 'And if you meet Erichtho, don't be scared. She will help you.'

You can now choose to go to the general treatment area (turn to **288**) or the resuscitation room (turn to **328**), but if you've had enough of this place, you can simply leave A&E and go up the stairwell (turn to **357**).

268

You enter the room and freeze. In the far corner, there is an old woman slumped on the bare frame of a bed. A tall, thin man is stood over her, one hand gripping her shoulder, a large book in his other. They don't seem to have noticed you. Just then, you feel a touch on your leg. You look down, then gasp and flinch away. The rag doll does the same. The walking, living rag doll. Its cloth arms are bent, holding cloth stumps to its painted-on mouth, then it bounds over to the sluice room. It pauses in the doorway, then nods encouragingly and points at a large machine inside. After a few seconds of you both staring at each other, the rag doll skips back to you and pushes against your legs, trying to move you towards the machine. It's weirdly strong for an inanimate toy. If you decide to do what the rag doll wants and go and look at the machine, turn to **339**, but if you'd prefer to talk to the man, turn to **170**.

269

Before your fingertips even touch the fine carving of this man's face, you sense a movement and flinch. You're not fast enough though, and the statue's hand grips your wrist like a vice. He bends down so he can stare into your eyes and says, 'Will my work never be done? Must I be plagued by these vermin; these witches?' Too late, you recall that Matthew Hopkins was a Witchfinder General. You try to tell him that you're not a witch, you're a nurse, but he snorts with disgust.

'I have heard that sorry excuse a hundred times. Just a healer? Never! You are in league with Satan and for that, you must die!' He grabs you now by the throat and lifts you clean off the floor. Your feet kick around frantically at first, but then weaker and weaker as you struggle for breath. You got further than most but still, your nightshift ends here.

270

Somehow, you feel more blind than you were before, as your vision struggles in the absence of the green light. Still, you're able to make your way through the archway and turn back into the pitch-black cave. Before long, your way is blocked by solid stone and you have to take a right turn. Keeping an almost constant contact with the wall, you slowly walk forward. Turn to **373**.

A few seconds later, you feel strong fingers prising your hands away and you realise that you still have hands. You look up into the face of the tall, thin man. He bends over and looks at you with black eyes. His beard, a mass of synthetic looking white curly hair, brushes against your face.

'Are you still hysterical?' he asks curiously, with a distinct German accent. You consider the question then shake your head. He smiles with relief. 'Good. I thought I was going to have to bash you with the book too.'

He tells you that he's Cornelius and leads you across the room towards the woman, but she screeches and shuffles backwards. Finally, she quietens and sits with her arms clutched around her legs, forehead resting on her knees and you can see clearly now, that she has had the top of her skull removed. You point with a shaking finger at the wrinkled, exposed brain.

'What happened to her?' you ask, feeling stupid because it's obvious what has happened to her.

'He calls her number 2, but she is Johanna. A powerful witch with a temper, but only with those who were cruel to others and did not heed her warning. She had a fierce ability to create madness and then *he* took it. I don't know how, but it was concentrated in the pineal gland, deep in the brain, and as you can see, he managed to gouge the gland out. Now all she can do is produce random chaos whenever she's frightened, so I stay with her. I protect her.' He smiles fondly at the witch and absent-mindedly strokes his wiry, white beard.

'All that with my hands in the machine — that was just a hallucination? She did that to me?' you splutter and Cornelius nods, begging you not to blame her, but blame the man who hurt her.

'Why doesn't somebody stop him then? Is he too strong?' you ask. Cornelius sighs gently and shakes his head. 'No, it just has to be the right person in the right place with the right knife.'

Your eyes widen and you hear Johanna whimper, then growl.

'He has to be stabbed?'

'No! Violence is not the answer. Johanna taught me that. No, people think witchcraft is potions, but they forget how powerful words can be. Obliterate the written name so no one can speak it ever again, then the life will be sucked from him. Obliterate the name!'

This talk of knives makes you look in your pocket, and you find the white-handled one that you'd grabbed from the macerator. Not all of it was madness then…

Before you can ask anything else, Johanna starts to rock back and forth and hit her fist against the jagged ridge of her skull. Abruptly, the shadows creep back and the room shifts with a kaleidoscope of colours. Cornelius pushes you to the door with a sharp 'Go!' and as you leave, you can hear him murmuring soothing words to the ruined witch.

Back in the corridor, you can enter the prayer room if you've not already been there (turn to **11**), but if you'd rather just carry on along the passageway, you can head left (turn to **113**) or right heading back towards the operating theatre department (turn to **338**).

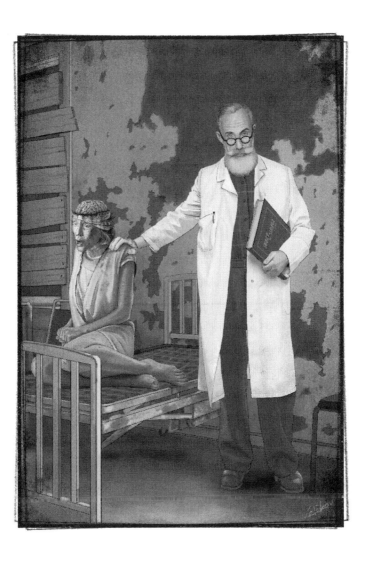

Taking a deep breath, you sink below the surface, then after a couple of heart beats, open your eyes. Directly above you is a face. You spasm and claw at the sides of the pool to drag yourself up, but two hands are pressing down on your shoulders and all you can do is wriggle like a hooked fish. The face stares down at you — alabaster skin and jet-black eyes studying you with a curious expression. Suddenly, it leans forward and sinks this face under the water. Your lungs are bursting and you're starting to see bright spots. The face is only inches away from yours and then it speaks,

'Back-to-front will help the nurse, read the letters in reverse.' The words ring clearly in your ears, then with a great slosh of water, the face and hands are gone.

You thrash upwards and drape yourself over the side, spluttering and coughing. You are alone in the room again, so get out of the pool with shaky legs and pull your scrubs back over your wet and shivery body. Still, as unpleasant as that was, you've got some valuable information. When you find an inscription that you think needs to be deciphered, simply reverse the alphabet so: A = Z, B = Y, C = X etc. You leave the room and head for the exit (turn to **171**).

273

You try the doors as you pass, but they are all locked until you reach the last one. There is no sound from within, but if you wish to enter this room, turn to **305**. However, if you decide that it isn't a good idea, you could head back to the junction (turn to **9**) or leave the ward via the door ahead of you (turn to **62**).

274

Back in the corridor, you find yourself at a junction where you can either head left, even though you don't know where it leads to (turn to **333**) or you could go straight on to the Sleep Disorders ward (turn to **163**).

275

Holding the candle high in the air and panicking as the noise from above becomes more agitated, you whisper the name Gaea. Nothing happens. You say it again, a little louder but not too loud, just in case… But nothing happens. You wait and then throw the candle back into the bag. Fat load of use that was! You carry on walking hoping that whatever is moving around up there, stays up there. Turn to **317**.

You walk cautiously, ducking your head every now and then to avoid the huge curtains of cobwebs hanging down. You can't begin to imagine what's happening and you have no idea what to do. All you do know is that you're being chased by a murderer and the only thing you can do is to try and find some help. You reach the end of the corridor and the double doors that take you to the main thoroughfare. You open them cautiously, expecting the maniac to jump out at you, but there's just more decay and silence. It feels as though you're the only person left alive. Where do you go now?

Left	Turn to **93**
Right	Turn to **242**

277

It's as though a battle is raging inside your body but after a minute, the oozing and throbbing stops and the fang wounds heal up again. Jezebeth looks angry — her plan to control you has been thwarted by the snake-skin bracelet. Now, you feel emboldened. It's time to strike back! Turn to **3**.

278

Incongruous in this Victorian setting, the door is locked with a similar-looking keypad to the one in the operating theatres. You don't know this code but nailed to the wall is a sepia page and you read:

> I am a 3-digit number.
> The second digit is 5 more than the third.
> The first is 8 less than the second.

If you can work out what the number is, turn to the section with the same number. If your brain can't get to grips with mathematics after all that's happened, you slump to the floor and cry. It would seem that you are going to be stuck here for a very long time.

279

You race across the room to the place where the door used to be. Screaming like a deranged person, you hurl yourself at the tapestry, using your weight to wrench it off the wall. It works. The fabric rips and falls gracefully to the floor. But there is only concrete behind it. Solid, cold, grey concrete. And definitely no door. You hear the cackling again and this time, all three women are laughing at you. Even the frog looks faintly amused. Dejected, you walk back to the one-eyed woman and nod in acquiescence. After all, you have no option now but to hear what she has to offer. Turn to **361**.

You wade cautiously through the sludge, half-expecting a swamp creature to coil around your ankle and drag you down, but the only attack comes from the insects that are breeding in the stagnant water. You feel them biting the side of your neck and slap them dead against your skin. You pass the door to the ground floor section of the operating theatres. It has a freshly painted symbol on it — an eight-spoked wheel. You are drawn to it and cross over, arm outstretched. But when you touch it, you realise that it's been drawn in blood. You wipe your fingers on your scrubs and try the doors. They're locked from the inside, as they normally are during the nightshift.

On the other side of the thoroughfare is a door leading to the laboratories. You've never been in there — why would you? — but if you'd like to investigate them now, turn to **34**. Otherwise, you have no choice but to carry on wading towards the end of the corridor. Turn to **256**.

You breathe a sigh of relief as you step into the pink corridor. Other than a persistent whistling noise, it seems peaceful, calm and, most importantly, pit-free. You walk along past the numerous closed doors until you reach a junction. You can either head left, which takes you out of the Ward (turn to **50**) or continue straight on (turn to **365**). Where do you go?

You feel pretty confident as you place the bluebell in its hand. After all, the Crow did say: 'All the Bs' and 'Give the flower, the beak to please' and surely, the beak is this figure and a flower with all the Bs has to be a bluebell. All you have to work out now is what the Crow meant by 'Tell the bees'… Your confidence is justified. The figure steps back with a sweep of his long coat and waves you in. Turn to **190**.

Initially, all you hear is a thin wheeze, but it's quickly followed by a light footstep, then the bucket is kicked out of the way. You remain motionless in the chair, head slumped to one side, keeping your breathing slow and steady. There's no more sound — whatever it is just stands there watching you. After a while, you feel an object being placed on your lap, followed by a 'tut' and then rapidly disappearing footsteps. You sit up and see the small copper cauldron in your lap, so you shout 'Hey' and 'Wait!' but they've gone. When you peer inside the cauldron, you see dried yellow flowers. You don't know if that's useful or not, but you decide to keep the cauldron safe in your bag for now, then leave this dank room. Turn to **368**.

You turn the handle and push open the door. It's dark inside and the strange sounds continue as if whatever is making the noise is unaware of your presence. You can see now that it's a padded cell. No furniture, no window, nothing. A cruel punishment for those caught in the grip of psychosis and not exactly the sort of thing to help them recover. At the far side of the cell, there is a body on the floor with someone crouched over it.

'Hello,' you call out and the figure turns around to face you. Your blood freezes as you see the hag clearly, her toothless mouth smeared with blackened blood. She's using her fingers to tear flesh off and is feeding on the corpse. She growls then starts to chant softly but threateningly. Her black, hooded eyes scowl and her claw-like fingernails draw patterns in the air. Is she casting a spell? You sense that you need to do something *right now* but what? You could attack her to prevent the spell from being completed (turn to **39**) or try to talk to her (turn to **348**).

You take another step backwards and feel the door handle against your hip. You reach around and in a swift movement, open the door, slide out and slam it behind you. The child screeches at you, sounding now like something bellowing from a deep pit in Hell rather than an innocent, young girl. The last thing you hear is the warning: 'Jezebeth knows what you are doing, and she is ready for you!' It chills your blood but at least you're back in the corridor.

You can either go left and exit the ward (turn to **62**) or head back to the junction (turn to **9**).

286

Charpentier studies the riddle and says 'I'm forbidden from telling you the answer, although it is perhaps the easiest I have ever seen and a child would be able to solve it. That said, I can give you a clue: the wood is used to make cricket bats.' With that, he sits down on the rug, tucks all four legs underneath his body and nods off.

Turn back to section **386** and try to answer the riddle.

287

He stares furiously at you, so you ask quietly, 'Is there anything I can help you with?' You're expecting him to throw something at you, so it's a surprise when he just jerks his head to the side. After the third time, you realise that he's gesturing behind the counter. You approach and glance over. Oh. Now you understand.

He's manacled to the counter by a rusty, thick chain. He's a prisoner here. He leans forward and hisses, 'Don't trust her, and whatever you do, don't go through the waiting area.' He looks directly at you with piercing eyes. Or are they mad eyes? What do you do now?

Go to the woman   Turn to **363**

Head off down the corridor   Turn to **260**

288

You drift around the trolleys and chairs and think about the myriad of people treated here. Most would have been patched up and sent home and some would have gone to the wards or even to you, for emergency operations. Over in the corner, there is a small plaster room with its white haze of Plaster of Paris over every surface. It even still hangs in the air and you can taste it in your mouth as every breath draws the gypsum into your lungs. You can't see anything of interest here so, feeling an irritated cough building up, you decide to leave. Just as you reach the door to leave, you spot something familiar hanging from a drip stand. A stethoscope. You grab it and drape it around your shoulders — you never know, it might come in handy. You can now choose to go to the quiet room (turn to **192**) or the resuscitation room (turn to **328**). However, if you've had enough of this place, you can simply leave A&E and go up the nearest stairwell (turn to **357**).

289

You go over to the young girl with red plaited hair and freckles. She is sat on the gurney, legs swinging and says,

'You look confused. Are you here to take my blood?' You shake your head, trying to make sense of it, but you can't even remember what you were thinking. It's like a fog is descending in your mind. You could leave the room right now (turn to **31**) or you could talk to the child and see if that helps (turn to **396**).

290

You believe that when he gathered the powers, he transformed and became a demon. And the only demon name you've heard in this place is Jezebeth. You scratch away at the word, wincing as the blade scrapes along the blackboard, until none of the name remains. You stand, head resting against the board, catching your breath in the silence. But then you hear his mocking words.

'You are stupid. For all your powers, you crones are so stupid.'

You turn slowly in disbelief — no! It can't be! But it is. Carmichael is still stood there and his assassin is blocking the exit. There is no way out for you and you tremble at what torture they have planned for you. Still, you can at least have the final word on one thing and with that decisive thought, you bring the knife down, stabbing straight through your left hand. Again and again until it is a pulp of ruined flesh.

'Try getting your power out of that now!' you screech and if you're lucky, this madness will protect you from truly knowing the horrors that await you.

291

You stand at the doorway to the Renal Unit and are about to turn the door handle when it's pulled open suddenly. Stood in front of you is a tall figure dressed in a long, waxed coat with a plague doctor mask on. If you've met this person before, turn to **314**. If this is the first time that you've met, turn to **27**.

292

You reach for the green-coloured chart, but the drawing pin falls out, taking the roster with it to the floor. You tut in annoyance, but then notice a small hole in the board. It had been hidden by the roster, and as you peer closer, you realise that the hole goes through the wall too! If you want to press your eye to the hole, so you can look through, turn to **46**. If you have a bad feeling about doing that and would rather just leave, turn to **162**.

293

You pour some of the fresh fountain water into the little copper cauldron, then set it over the fire. It heats up and simmers for a few minutes, steeping the yellow flowers. If you want to use this mixture now as a compress, turn to **298**. However, if you're feeling thirsty, you could just drink it as a tea (turn to **251**).

294

You crouch down by Nathanael's chair, almost asphyxiated by the stench of ammonia. Poor man, you think, does this nurse do nothing for them?

'Excuse me, sir, can you tell me anything?'
Nathanael points a shaking finger at the far wall. You turn to look but it's just yellow. You're not sure what it means and when you turn back, his head has sagged against his chest. You stand up, ready to go, but then he mutters, 'It's a type of tree.' You wait but those words

of wisdom are the only thing he says, so you leave the day room (turn to **201**).

295

You go over to the polished and ornately carved sideboard on which the crystal decanter and matching tumblers stand. You can't deny it, you are tempted to sample what looks like brandy, but you know better than to trust anything here. At that moment, you catch sight of your reflection in the surface of the varnished wood. Your face is now a skull with huge, black, empty eye sockets and long, curved fangs. You scream and jump back, feeling your face to reassure yourself that you don't actually look like that. What was it? A premonition? A warning? Who knows and right now, you don't really care — you've had enough — time to get out!

You pick up the box, tuck it under your arm, then, taking a deep breath, push through the mirror again. Turn to **10**.

296

You rattle the small pewter bell and its delicate tinkling sound can barely be heard in the pharmacy. Feeling stupid, you put it down on the counter with a tinny clatter and contemplate giving a bellow of 'Jezebeth' — maybe just shouting the demon's name will work — but then you sense a shifting in the atmosphere and turn around to face this presence. Jezebeth has arrived. Turn to **149**.

Your instinct is to cheerily announce yourself, but your smile freezes when you enter the bedroom. What you see on the bed is possibly the most ghoulish thing you've ever witnessed. The bottom of the bed might look normal, but the head is anything but. Its scalp has been cut and pulled down over the face and the skull has been removed, exposing the brain. There are countless EEG electrodes inserted directly into the grey matter, but the horror is the cat who is perched nonchalantly on the patient's chest and appears to be trying to eat pieces of brain tissue.

Do you pick up anything nearby and throw it at the cat (turn to **59**), try to get rid of the cat, so you can examine the dead person (turn to **376**) or leave the room in disgust (turn to **126**)?

You make the compress and press it to your neck, sighing as the warm chamomile relaxes and soothes your tight muscles. After fifteen minutes, you feel ready to carry on. You realise that the dogs have stopped barking and there seems to be nothing else here in the garden, so you head back inside and continue along the corridor. Turn to **301**.

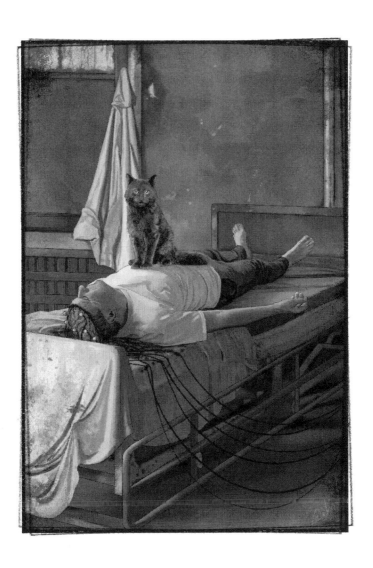

299

At the end, the corridor turns again to the right and you realise that you've come full circle — back to where you started! The Vascular ward lies directly ahead with its door slightly ajar. Turn to **380** if you want to investigate, but if you'd rather head for stairwell A now and go downstairs, turn to **323**.

300

You creep cautiously forward and with every step, pause to listen for movement ahead. But there is only silence. Eventually, you peer around the corner and gasp as you see the pit right in front of you. Deep, steep and practically filling the corridor. If you'd have run around, you would've fallen straight into it! You blow out a sigh of relief then think about what to do next. You could return back down the corridor until you reach the junction in the x-ray department again (turn to **56**) or you could carefully make your way around the edge of the pit and continue towards the Children's Ward (turn to **224**).

301

The claustrophobic feeling inside this papery passageway intensifies with every step, so you're relieved to see the exit ahead of you but then you notice another door on your left. Through a crack in the pages, you can see the shimmering reflection of light off water — it's the birthing pool. You enter into a blue-green room, free of words and pages, and it could be relaxing, if you like the impression of being underwater, but the humidity is too oppressive to be comfortable. You go over to the pool and dangle your fingers into the water. It's warm and looks clean. The temptation to get into this giant bath is great but is that the most sensible thing to do in this situation? If you decide to throw caution to the wind, strip off and get into the pool, turn to **131**. If you think it might be safer to stay on dry land but wash your face, turn to **24**. If these options don't appeal, you can just exit the room and leave the department (turn to **171**).

If you decide to throw caution to the wind, strip off and get into the pool, turn to **131**. If you think it might be safer to stay on dry land but wash your face, turn to **24**. If these options don't appeal, you can just exit the room and leave the department (turn to **171**).

302

You think this is where the Crow told you to go but it spoke so quickly, you're not really sure. After a couple more steps, you spot a piece of glass on the floor and have an overwhelming compulsion to pick it up. You grasp it tightly in your hand, wincing as it slices the skin but are completely unable to let it go. Almost as if you are watching someone else, you see your own hand raise the shard and cut around your hairline. Your other hand reaches up and grabs hold of the skin edges and you start to flay your own face off. The pain is unimaginable, but you can't stop. It's as though someone else is controlling you. Blood pours down as you cast aside the mask-like skin and start on your chest. Death will come eventually, but you'll still have plenty of time to wonder what went wrong.

303

Looking surreptitiously around to see if Empusa is watching, you sneak over to the fridge with the red flashing light. There's not much difference between the cold emanating from within the fridge and the icy atmosphere of the cave, but instantly, you can see that the fridge is not just full of blood bags. There is a thick, cream candle perched on one of the shelves. If you have room in your bag, you can choose to take it with you. Make a note of your decision, then leave the blood bank. Turn to **270**.

304

You walk down the corridor until you come to a heavy door. You enter and go past familiar signs — nuclear medicine, CT scan, MRI — which look strange next to the Victorian architecture and furnishings. You come to a junction with a right turn, which takes you towards the children's ward. If you want to go there, turn to **115**. Otherwise, you can continue straight on to the rest of the x-ray department (turn to **204**).

305

You walk into a small treatment room with a gurney on one side and a desk on the other, and there is someone sat on the gurney. Have you recorded the word CLONE during your travels? If you have, turn to **90**, but if you haven't, turn to **289**.

306

You find yourself back in the blue corridor. Just ahead is the entrance to the Recovery bay and a little further on is the staircase, which leads downstairs to more operating theatres. You want to get out of this oppressive darkness, so if you decide to try your luck downstairs, turn to **388**. If you'd prefer to head to the Recovery area, turn to **117**.

307

You examine the bottles of soap, knowing that Lister saved countless lives by using antiseptics to prevent infections. When you look at the fourth bottle, you can see a tiny wedge of cardboard protruding from behind it. Gripping it with your nails, you give a tug and find yourself holding a dried and pressed bluebell. You can't imagine how it could be of any use but still, you carefully place it in your pocket and head for the exit. Turn to **8**.

308

The room is minimalist and modern. In the centre is a dentist's chair, with the sterile, high-tech instruments, suction and lights attached. There is a small cough from behind and you whirl around startled. A woman is stood there regarding you with a cool, appraising eye. The dentist, you presume.

'Sit,' she orders. You feel a tingle of nerves in your stomach. You really don't want to sit in any dentist's chair, but she's standing so close, you do as she says — if only to get her out of your space. She then tuts loudly and shakes her head.

'Think about it! If the witch you asked was the liar, the other would tell the truth about the door but the answer the liar gives would be the wrong door. If the witch you asked was the truth-teller, the other one would lie and say the wrong door, but the answer would have to be that. Either way, if you ask for the safe door, they would always point to the *wrong* door.' It takes you a while to follow her logic, but the realisation finally sinks in. You should've picked the other door.

With a jolt of fear, you try to launch out of the chair, but your arms are already tightly restrained by two thick leather straps. The dentist picks up the drill and approaches you, grabbing your jaw and forcing your head back. You twist and arch, but you're trapped and you're not going to be able to escape — your nightshift ends here. The whirring gets closer and closer and then you hear the concentrated murmur of the dentist in your ear,

'Of course, we won't be using anaesthesia….'

309

'About bloody time too!' says Charpentier, standing up on the patient's chest, giving a full body shake then leaping effortlessly off the bed. He does a fluid figure of eight around your legs then looks up.

'I can help you. Not with the killing, that's down to you, but I have learnt a thing or two about this place.' You accept his offer, although you're not convinced he can be trusted. Still, the company will be nice.

If you find yourself at a section that has an asterisk, **subtract 100** and go to the new section to see what advice Charpentier has for you.

You both head for the door, leaving the poor patient on the bed.

'What about him?' you ask. Charpentier looks at you as if you are the biggest idiot he's ever seen.

'He's dead. He's not going to mind if I leave.' You follow him out with a very confused expression on your face. Turn to **126**.

310

It looks like it's a maintenance tunnel. Above your head there's a variety of PVC and foil-clad pipes. Why it opens up into the Special Care Baby Unit is anyone's guess and for that matter, who knows where you're going to end up! You carry on walking down the sloping passageway, wrapping your arms tightly around your body in a futile attempt to stay warm. The corridor then takes a left turn and seems to be rising again too. You keep going because you don't really have any other choice, and this seems to be paying off — in the distance the light gets brighter and you soon arrive at a junction. To the left is a corridor heading to another department with blue flowers strewn around its entrance, and straight ahead, the passageway continues to a plain white door with the Bowl of Hygieia painted on it. You head this way. Turn to **36**.

Making your way back down the corridor, you think about where you could go now. It's not a simple case of getting help anymore; you need to find out what the Hell is going on. That is if you live long enough to do that! Talking of which, you slow down as you reach the junction. What if he's got out? What if he's waiting for you? You peer around the corner and your heart stops. The door back to the operating theatres is wide open. Adrenalin floods your body and you freeze, but gradually, you start to process what you're seeing. In particular, that the place you've worked in for years, doesn't look quite as you remember it. If you decide to investigate further and head back into the operating theatres, turn to **332**. However, if you want to head left towards the main hospital thoroughfare, turn to **276**.

You put the last key into its lock and hold your breath. Turn to **15**.

The demon stands before you, swaying slightly from side to side on a thick serpent body. The scales are a dull taupe colour but with shimmering edges of amber. The torso and head are that of a skeleton, albeit one with dried and leathery flesh tightly gripping the bones underneath. Her eyes are huge black holes and the jaw contains fiercely sharp snake fangs. A voice fills your head, although you don't see Jezebeth mouthing any words. You are practically numb with fear, listening to the confident and condescending laugh as the demon appraises you. If you have a snake bite wound on your hand, turn to **185**. If you don't, turn to **238**.

314

Despite the leather beak, you can still hear the impatient 'huff' as the figure looks at you.

'Not you again! Well?' As before, it puts out a hand, palm up. This time, you're prepared but which item do you put into its hand?

Obsidian amulet	Turn to **57**
Dried bluebell	Turn to **282**
Crushed sea eagle talons	Turn to **169**

315

Putting the sickly-yellow colour behind you, you wonder what to do now. You could investigate the bathroom if you haven't done so already (turn to **337**) or else you can head to the ward exit (turn to **172**).

316

You approach the bag gingerly, watching as it continues to shift and squirm. Do you reach into the bag, pulling out the sheets until you find whatever this is (turn to **176**) or knock the bag over and shake the contents out onto the floor (turn to **32**)?

317

Slowly, you creep forward placing each foot carefully and as silently as possible. The noise from above though, grows and becomes more threatening. You can barely breathe because of the tension when suddenly, there is a calamitous cacophony and the cavern is filled with the sound of thousands of wings beating. You dart forward in an attempt to outrun them, but you are immediately surrounded by a flurry of feathers and the sharp jabs of large beaks. You drop to your knees and try to cover your face and eyes. Just when it seems that the pain is never-ending, it stops. Turn to **49**.

318

You reply that you'll answer her riddle and are slightly unnerved by the mischievous expression on the washerwoman's face. What are you getting yourself into? She pulls a piece of chalk from the pocket of her pinafore and writes a series of numbers on the floor.

'All you need to do is tell me what comes next and then I'll tell you something useful.'

The numbers are: 4, 7, 15, 29, 59, 117... If you think you know the answer, turn to the section with the same number as the missing part of the sequence. If you can't work it out, you just have to leave the washerwoman and her riddle behind (turn to **79**).

319

You pull back the sheet and wince at the sight of the corpse. It looks like the post-mortem was interrupted because the ribcage is pulled apart and the thorax is empty. But where were the organs, you think, looking around the otherwise spotless mortuary. Never mind. You replace the sheet and head for the exit door. Time to explore what else was down here. You didn't even know there was a basement and definitely have never been down here before. You've taken only a few steps when you hear a noise from behind. You spin around and scream uncontrollably, sensing a warm wetness spread out down your thighs. The corpse is standing in front of you, the sheet pooled around its feet. It staggers forward, arms outstretched. You could run but you can't. You can't even breathe, so great is your fear. Its hands encircle your back, dragging you close. You can hear it grunting with the effort, although, without lungs, you're not sure how it's doing that. As it starts to feed on your flesh, pulling great chunks off and swallowing them whole, you're certain you can hear it mutter again and again: 'Praise be to Baigujing for this meal'.

320

You exit the golden chamber and walk back down the panelled passageway to the pharmacy. You are carrying your strange brew and carefully place it on the apothecary counter. There's no backing down now. It's time to face Jezebeth. If you have a small pewter bell, turn to **296**. If you don't, turn to **51**.

321

You put the last key into its lock and hold your breath. Turn to **15**.

322

It is a formidable, thick steel door with no sign to say what lies beyond. To the side of the frame, is a 3-digit combination lock and above that, a hole in the brickwork. If you want to delve your hand into the hole and have a rummage about, turn to **116**, but if that sounds like a recipe for disaster, you should go back to the junction (turn to **210**).

323

The stairwell is in a U-shape, circling a lift shaft. As you take the first turn, you gasp and recoil. There is a skeleton — a human skeleton — slumped on the steps, curled up in the foetal position. You wonder briefly what happened to the person that they died here like that but sidle quickly past the white bones. You step into the wide corridor of the main thoroughfare, grimacing as a splash of thick green pond water soaks into your socks. As far as you can see, the entire place looks flooded and the air is heavy with the stagnant odour

So, where to now? You could head left to the Accident and Emergency department (turn to **146**) or go right towards the main entrance and the rest of the hospital (turn to **280**).

324

Once you've got the trapdoor open, you can see a rickety ladder that takes you down into a musty chamber. A dark, heavy drape covers an archway which seems to be the only way out. You gingerly pull it to the side and gape with shock at what you see.

Considering the caves and concrete you've just passed through, you weren't expecting to chance upon the warmest, most opulent looking room that you've ever seen. The walls are a deep indigo, as are the chairs, sofa and rugs. It's a study with a huge oak writing desk taking up centre stage and sat at it, is a round-faced, bouncy looking witch. Her face is ruddy which could be due to the crackling fire in the hearth or the half-drunk glass of wine perched on the desk. She beams with delight and, throwing her arms wide, cries 'Welcome' then gestures you to the nearest chair. You sit down, unsure what to make of this. Luckily, she talks enough for both of you, although her words don't give much comfort.

'You are so close to danger; I can't believe you don't taste the peril. Wrong decisions and wrong routes. Creeping closer and closer, she nearly has you and when she strings you up, you won't be cut free, oh no.'

You have no idea what she's talking about, but it doesn't sound good. The witch plants her hands decisively on her thighs, nods at you and continues,

'Well, at least you had the good fortune to cross my path. I sit here writing down all my knowledge in the hope that it could save us and now it's time to practise what we preach.' She looks at you, with a hopeful expression. 'I don't suppose you've seen my Book of Shadows, have you?' What's your answer?

Yes, I have it here   Turn to **342**
No, I've not seen it   Turn to **181**

325

You rummage around in the bag and eventually find the small petri dish with the chalky grey-white powder. It looks a little disappointing now but, as you hold it in your palm, the pink luminescence gets brighter and brighter until you have to shut your eyes. And with it, you can hear a flapping of wings; louder and louder until you have to raise your arms, wrapping them around your head. You're sure that you are surrounded by a flock of birds but then, they are gone. It is silent. You open your eyes and to your amazement, you're sat back in the corridor near the edge of the pit. You scramble up and back away. The only option now is the Children's Ward, so you open the door (turn to **281**).

It's as though a battle is raging inside your body but after a minute, the oozing and throbbing stops and the fang wounds heal up again. Jezebeth looks angry — her plan to control you has been thwarted by the snake-skin bracelet and now, you feel emboldened. It's time to strike back! Turn to **220**.

You remember the phrase clearly: 'Be with the corpse behind the number of ribs.' It's not rocket science. Twelve pairs of ribs equal 24, so you open the fridge door but are surprised to see a shrouded body already in there. Did you forget your anatomy lessons? You don't think so and decide to crawl in. The door slams shut, locking you in this absolute darkness and a wave of claustrophobia swells inside. You try to stay calm and focused on getting to the far side of the compartment, although you have no idea what that's going to achieve. With metaphorical fingers crossed, you finally reach the end and push the wall of the fridge. Nothing happens. Tears flood your eyes and you give a desperate, harder push. It works! Light bursts in as the wall silently swings open and before it can close again, you scramble forward to get out. At the last second, you sense movement and the corpse grabs your wrist. You tug frantically, hysteria rising, then you realise that it isn't trying to drag you back in; it simply wants to give you something. You see the photograph in its other hand and stop pulling.

'For me?' It waves the photograph at you in answer and you gingerly take it. The corpse slumps again, all trace of animation gone. You finally leave the fridge and find yourself in a room full of industrial-sized dryers. Turn to **262**.

328

This is where doctors and nurses strived to snatch people back from the jaws of death. It was a place of high drama and emotion.

'And high energy,' a voice says from the far corner. At first you think it's just a shadow yet the smell is strong. It's a delicious smell of cooked meat but with a surge of nausea, you see that it's cooked *flesh*. Human flesh. It's not a shadow; it's a charred human being, which is still smoking yet still walking. Walking towards you! Should you leave?

'Don't leave,' it says, and you realise it's read…

'Reading your mind? Yes.' It stops and stands in front of you. You can clearly see the tightened and split skin and the darkened, empty pits where eyes once were. The stench is nauseating.

'I'm number 7.' She gestures as if she were pulling back her hair to show off the side of her head, but there's no hair left, just blackened scalp. 'Carmichael took my ears because he needed my power. He forgot though. There are more ways to skin a cat and witches are resourceful. Vengeful too. He should not forget that!'

'So if he took your ears, how can you still hear thoughts?' you ask, wondering if this night could get any more surreal. It raises its arms out to the side, making an horrendous crackling noise as the too-tight flesh gives way and rents.

'The answer is around you. Colour is more powerful than you could ever believe. Orange stimulates energy. All you need is to learn how to harness it'

'But does that mean you can't leave here?' It acknowledges your question with a sad nod of the head, then looks up and takes a step towards you.

'But you can. You need to save yourself and by doing that, you can save me and my 10 sisters. He hides beyond this place and you can only leave through the mortuary.'

You look totally bemused and are about to say 'What?', when it reaches out and silences you with a finger on your lips, before stating dramatically: 'Be with the corpse behind the number of ribs. Now GO.' With that shout, she pushes you back and disappears, leaving you with barbecued grease on your lips.

Once you've wiped that off, you need to decide where to go next. You can now choose to go to the general treatment area (turn to **288**) or the quiet room (turn to **192**), or if you've had enough of this place, you can simply leave A&E and go up the stairwell (turn to **357**).

Your head sinks into the downy pillow and you fall into a deep sleep. When you awake, you have no idea how much time has passed, but you feel miraculously rejuvenated. You stretch, sit up and see the ghost perched next to you. It is wearing ragged, grey clothes and is silently wailing. It stops as it realises that you're looking at it, although its mouth remains gaping open. It reaches a grey hand out, and you just frown and shake your head in confusion. What does it want from you? In response, it leans back and starts the silent wailing again. Suddenly, unseen hands press you back down onto the bed, and the pillow is pushed down on your face. It's suffocating you! You thrust your bag at it — take what you want, you think — and to your absolute relief, the pillow is removed. You gasp and breathe heavily, but the ghost is still sat there and your bag is untouched. It holds its hand out again.

'What do you want?' you ask, getting annoyed now. It simply bows its head and looks depressed.

'Am I supposed to know what you want or do you want me to choose?' you snap. With the latter suggestion, the ghost perks up and looks hopeful. It thrusts its hand out a little more.

Choose any item from your bag and give it to the ghost. It doesn't matter what it is, the ghost will be pleased to get anything, but make a note of the object you have lost. You get up now and decide to explore the ward. If you choose to go to the bathroom, turn to **217**, but if you'd prefer to inspect the day room, turn to **112**.

330

You say the name and the lab technician winces, then shushes you.

'Not so loud,' he says. 'You never know who's listening.'

'I know he's a killer and he takes body parts!'

'Not just any parts though. Special ones. Why do you think he took the intestines? It's all linked. Guts move stuff from one place to another and that's the power he wants. To relocate from one place to another. Different organs have different powers. There's 12 in all. He needs all 12. I've said too much.'

With a panicked shake of the head, he turns, then pauses and reaches into his pocket. He brings out a delicate silver chalice and puts it into your hands, saying, 'You'll need this more than I will!' then disappears rapidly up the stairs. Stunned, you replay his words in your mind — 12 in all, so did the number 5 where the guts were draped mean that he'd already got 5? And power? Really? Surely this Robert Carmichael was simply a deranged and deluded psychopath! You consider chasing after the lab technician, but instead, you pocket the chalice and carry on down the stairs. Turn to **222**.

331

You cautiously press your fingertips against the mirror. It feels like a normal mirror, but just as you start chastising yourself for being gullible, there's a give in the surface and your hand slips through. With a shrug of shoulders, you think, 'What the Hell!' and lift your leg up to step across. Turn to **234**.

Strangely, the first thing you notice is that the normally polished floor is covered with a thin carpet of green mould and there are no footprints smeared into it. So wherever you were earlier, it certainly wasn't here. Which hopefully means that *he* isn't here too. The walls used to be a pale green colour but now are painted a dark Prussian blue. It's discoloured and flaking in places but still feels like being in a deep abyss. The watery sensation is enhanced by a constant trickling ahead of you in the corridor, but it smells unusual and distinctly acidic. You're not sure what you should do. This obviously isn't the way back to your world but where is? With an impatient shake, you decide that standing here isn't going to help. You need to find something out. Anything! You start walking down the corridor past the operating theatres, when you notice one of the doors is propped open and there's a light on. There wasn't a light on before…

If you want to enter the operating theatre, turn to **22**. If you'd prefer to investigate the acidic smell, turn to **153**.

333

Soon, the corridor takes a right turn and before long, you arrive at a large foyer. Turn to **108**.

334

You whisper 'mite' and wait. Nothing. You say it more assertively. Nothing. You tilt your head back and proclaim it loudly. Nothing. You stare at the portrait and will something to happen, but… nothing. You give up and, feeling a bit stupid, head to the crossroads. Turn to **216**.

335

You step out onto the grass and the scent of jasmine in the fresh air is beguiling. You lift your face up to the sun, seeing that the storm clouds have quickly passed by. It's a beautiful, peaceful place, but then you see a cluster of gravestones underneath a tree and a woman resting back against the gnarly trunk. She beckons you over. She looks kind, but did that mean anything in this place? And the dogs were ominously silent now. If you decide to go over and sit next to the woman, turn to **29**. If you decide that this is a trap, you can quickly leave and head back to the corridor (turn to **301**).

336

No doubt, this is a very strange pattern on the floor. A three-legged, curvy shape. You look up, shielding your eyes as best you can, but you can't see what is casting this shadow. You look down again and a disembodied voice says, 'A triskele can represent the maiden, the mother and the crone.'

You look around wildly, shouting, 'Who's there?' There is silence for the longest time, then the voice replies.

'You will fear the crone, but she will be your helping hand.'

Well, you don't seem to be under attack and you feel like you should say something portentous to that, but you can't think of anything, so you just say thanks. A spider scuttles down the nearby wall and disappears into a crack in the skirting board. Was that who…? No, surely not. You shake your head and carry on to the end of the corridor. It turns sharply to the left and you follow it around. Turn to **81**.

337

You stand in the doorway and, for a second, think that there's nothing here. Just an old tin bath and a wooden bucket. Something makes you step a little further though, and then you see the water, which is filling the bath and the naked old woman lying under the surface. Her eyes and her mouth are gaping open and when you touch the water, you recoil at how cold it is. Suddenly, the old woman locks her eyes on you and sits up. The icy water splashes you and her frozen hand grips your arm like a clamp.

'Did you think I'd drowned?' she asks, 'Did you?' You nod frantically, still trying to prise her fingers off your arm.

'How can I drown if I have no lungs?' She says almost triumphantly, as if she'd won some bet or game. With that, she lets go of you and slumps against the back of the tub, gazing at you with bored eyes. You're getting used to this now, so you ask the obvious question.

'Did Carmichael take your lungs?' The old woman snorts at the name and nods.

'What power did he get from them?' You continue, curious now rather than scared.

'I had the power of levitation and he called me number 9. People started making up stories about witches flying around on broomsticks but that was just nonsense. Can you imagine trying to balance on a broomstick? Of course not! It's too thin for a start. Ridiculous. But we can levitate, and I suppose some careless old witch let herself be seen and that's where the tales came from. Next thing you know, we're fornicating with Satan and being burnt. Or hanged. Or drowned.' With the final word, she slaps both hands against the water's surface in frustration.

'I am trying to stop all this,' you tell her. 'but is there anything I can do now to help you?' Although she shakes her head sulkily, she pats your arm for this kindness.

'Just remember that if you're concocting any spells or potions, the cup or container you mix everything in is just as important as the ingredients themselves. It's usually specific to the spell but as a rule of thumb, you can't go wrong with silver.' With that, she slips back under the water to resume her icy vigil.

You leave the bathroom and can go to the day room if you haven't been there already (turn to **58**) or head to the ward exit (turn to **172**).

338

You arrive back at the corner, where the corridor turns left again and takes you back to where you started. Directly ahead is the entrance to stairwell B, and even from this distance you can see the pentacle daubed on the door. That cannot be a good sign. Against your better judgement, you inch forward and reach out for the handle but surprisingly, it won't shift. It's locked. The Renal Unit is on your right but to be honest, you've had enough. You make your way quickly to the other stairs and head to the ground floor (turn to **323**).

339

You enter the sluice room, which is dwarfed by the large, old-fashioned macerator. You couldn't even begin to imagine how many cardboard urinal bottles and vomit bowls ended up being destroyed inside that. The hatch is open and you peer inside. It looks like a huge blender with fierce blades and…what's that? The rag doll jumps up and down excitedly. That's what it wanted you to find. There's something wedged underneath one of the blades and if you want to reach in to grab it, turn to **16**. If you think that's the worse idea in the history of bad ideas, you can just quickly leave this room and go to talk to the man and woman (turn to **170**).

340

It's so soothing that you keep drifting off, bobbing gently around in the water. Sometimes, you think that you can hear a voice trying to get your attention, but when you concentrate, there's nothing. You must be imagining it. After half an hour of wallowing, you reluctantly get out and pull your scrubs on over your wet body. It was worth it though. You needed some time to recharge if you're going to get through this. Shivering slightly, you leave the room and head for the exit (turn to **171**).

341

You sit and sigh, as the tension drains out of your muscles. The thought occurs to you that this could be a mistake — what if you fall asleep and someone gets you? — but it's fleeting. You look around and wonder about all the patients that have sat in this plastic (plastic? In a Victorian hospital?) chair and waited on tests that could bring them dreaded news. Your eyes fall upon an old newspaper. The date is November 9th, 1888 and there is a crossword puzzle blazoned across the page. Were crosswords even invented in 1888?. Never mind. There is one clue still to be filled in. 10 across. 5 letters. Well-defined portions of an organ. Mmm. ____ / __O__ / ____ / __E__ / __S__

What is the answer?

Nodes   Turn to **353**

Lobes   Turn to **241**

Pores   Turn to **91**

342

You pull the heavy tome from your bag and hand it over to the witch, who clasps her hands together and lets out a sob. She reaches for the burgundy book, which starts to vibrate again in excitement. It seems to be pleased to be back with its author. She holds the book to her chest then gives you a weepy smile. 'Thank you,' she says, as she places it on the desk then stands up. She sweeps over to the far wall, mutters some words that you can't make out and beckons you over.

'You must take this passageway. It's the only way to survive now and it's all I can do to help you.' She shoves you decisively in the back and you stumble forward. You raise your hands and cry out, anticipating a nasty bruising as you collide with the wall. Except the wall isn't there anymore. You're in a round, indigo tunnel — it's almost like being inside a huge vein — and the round witch and her comfy study have gone. You have no option but to follow this snaking tunnel wherever it goes. Turn to **156**.

343

You step into the foyer and stride to the exit. You feel almost exhilarated, although you're not exactly sure what you'll do once you're out of this stinking cesspool. Still, cross that bridge and all that! Grasping the handles, you dramatically open the double doors and…
Your vision narrows as you teeter on the brink of passing out, feeling like you've been punched in the gut. A brick wall! There's no way out; it's just a brick wall. You sink to your knees, tears pooling in your eyes, but

after a few minutes, you get up. Well, what else can you do?

You turn back around and take a deep, steadying breath. The cafeteria and Information Desk are on your right and whilst the whole area looks deserted, it is very messy with mounds of litter and discarded polystyrene piled up on plastic tables. If you want to explore the cafeteria and risk whatever is buried in those mounds, turn to **180**, however, if you'd prefer to go to the Information Desk, turn to **239**.

344

You stride around the corner dramatically, almost saying 'Ta da!' to announce yourself. It has the intended effect as the two young women on the stairs freeze and stare at you. They are wearing a uniform of a long, dark blue dress with a cotton pinafore and white cap and their skin has a slight grey sheen to it.

Only now do you start to wonder what you should say, but that is a moot point. The women fade before your eyes, and even though you shout 'Wait!', they disappear. There's nothing else to do but go down the stairs, and at the bottom you reach a locked door. Turn to **278**.

With a heavy thud, the door unlocks, but you have to really shove it to open it and then you step into a dark and gloomy passageway. There are numerous doors with iron bars across the small observation windows. It looks like a prison, but you think this actually might have been the psychiatric ward. Of course, the intention was never about making them better; it was about keeping them away from the 'normal' people.

You walk along the corridor and see the remnants of iron bed frames in cold, depressing rooms. Finally, you reach a junction. Leading straight on, the corridor just seems to have more of these cell-like rooms, so you decide to take the left turn instead. There's nothing of interest here too and eventually, you come to the exit. If you want to leave the asylum, turn to **227**. However, there is a closed door to your left and you can hear a strange noise coming from within. If you want to see what's happening in there, turn to **284**.

The footsteps get closer and closer and suddenly, a figure bursts through the far door into the ward. You gasp, which makes it stop in its tracks. For a split second, you both stare at each other — doppelgängers — and then it dives into the last room on the left. With your heart pounding, you try to make sense of this but there is no explanation you can think of. Make a note of the codeword **CLONE**.

You tentatively walk forward, curiosity getting the better of you, but as you reach a junction, you pass a room on the right and hear the soft voices of children from inside. Do you:

Enter the room on the right?	Turn to **182**
Walk to the last room on the left?	Turn to **273**
Go to the junction and turn right?	Turn to **50**

347

You feel relieved as the door closes behind you on the red room, but you know the time has come to stop putting off the inevitable and face your fears. You head to the door straight ahead — the mortuary. Turn to **6**.

348

'Stop, please,' you cry, 'I need to end all of this, so I can go home! Can you help me?'

The crone stops her muttering and finger waving and regards you, her head tilted to one side.

'Do you know *who* you need to destroy?' she asks, although it's difficult to understand her because of the damaged mouth.

'I think it was Robert Carmichael, but I keep hearing about Jezebeth too. I'm confused. Are they different people or is it two names for the same person?'

The crone smiles and bares her gums. You flinch but don't feel so scared by her anymore.

'That depends on who you talk to. If you asked Carmichael, he would say that *he* is Jezebeth. That when he took my teeth and my power of resurrecting the dead, he ascended to the demonic realm.' She laughs, shaking her head then continues, 'But if you asked Jezebeth, she would tell you that Carmichael is her toy. He believes simply what Jezebeth wants him to believe.'

'So I have to kill Jezebeth then?'

The crone hisses at you and throws a blood clot into the corner of the room. You draw back, wondering what you've said to upset her.

'You don't kill demons, you fool! You destroy them. You must destroy Jezebeth. But don't forget Carmichael. He may be a man, but they can be dangerous beasts too. You must kill him before he rips you apart.'

Great, you think. Just when you thought one murder was pushing it, it turns out you have to do two! So where do you go from here? Before you can even think about that though, the crone creeps closer towards you. With her green skin and rotting stench, she is your worst nightmare come to life, but you resist shaking her off when she grabs your leg and whispers,

'Do you want to know how to destroy Jezebeth?'

You nod, even though demon destroying is the last thing you want to be doing. The crone rears up suddenly, taller and straighter than you thought possible and shouts,

'Then you will have to prove your worthiness!'

If you want to take her test and find out how to destroy the demon, turn to **68**. If you think you've found out enough and just want to leave this room and its foul occupants, turn to **227**.

'Just like Carmichael!' she shouts, violently slamming her fist down on the bed. The flies rise up, irritated by this disturbance, and swirl about your head. 'All you lot ever care about is the power. You're either scared of it, so you kill us or you want it, so you kill us. Well, not again!' You try to answer, to reassure her that you're not like that; you just want to go home, but the flies are everywhere, buzzing in your ears, blacking out your vision and getting in your mouth. You swat desperately, spinning around and in all this chaos, you don't notice the strings emerging from your wrists, knees and head. Slowly, the flies settle back down and then you realise just how heavy your limbs are. You turn to look but your head has a jerky, wobbling motion that you can't control. You do get a glimpse though, a fleeting glance of your polished wooden arms. Upsetting Gretl, the puppet master, was not a wise move. She will keep you on a tight rein from now on, as her latest marionette.

With your nose only inches away, you can clearly see the pores, hair follicles and a hundred different shades of skin, but the tattoos are particularly poignant. You wonder about the people who sat through the inking, never knowing that they'd end up in some macabre display. You see a bunch of green shamrocks, a red banner warning 'Beware of foxes and Baigujing', a delicate fairy with gossamer wings and gothic handwriting proclaiming: Meine Haut ist mein Grimoire.

After studying the stretched skin though, you still have no idea what's going on, so you turn your back on the barrier and think about where to go next. Do you head:

Straight on?	Turn to **226**
Left?	Turn to **125**

351

You yank the door handle down and pull desperately but it's locked fast. His shadow looms over and you turn screaming. You put your hands up, but he is too strong, and the knife is too sharp. Mercifully, darkness takes you and your end is over quickly.

352

Briefly, you wonder if crawling on your hands and knees would be safer, but that's probably a very bad idea. Instead you inch along, groping around for any obstacles and testing each step, in case the floor isn't there. It takes ages, although you probably haven't gone far when you start to hear a gentle humming and see an eerie green light. Maybe your eyes are playing tricks as a result of the sensory deprivation, but if you want to investigate the light and humming, turn to **64**. If you'd prefer to keep going and not risk getting lost in here, turn to **261**.

353

You pluck your trusty biro out of a pocket and scribble in the missing letters N and D. As you turn the page, an advert catches your eye. It's a Victorian man complete with stovepipe hat and extravagant moustache, but his entire body is a carrot. Apparently, this is meant to entice you to buy seeds. You raise your eyebrows at how bizarre it is. The rest of the newspaper is just more adverts, obituaries and local stories, and you can't escape the fact that you're now prevaricating. With a sigh, you put the newspaper down and instantly it's engulfed in a golden flame. You gasp, leaping onto your feet, away from the burning mass. Soon, all that remains are the black wisps of paper, which float slowly down like snowflakes. You can now leave the department either by the way you entered (turn to **17**) or the opposite exit (turn to **208**), or if you haven't yet tried the door with the red warning light and would like to do so now, turn to **75**.

354

You open the doors and leave the x-ray department. The corridor doesn't seem as bright as it did earlier, and you can see dark clouds gathering in the sky. That probably doesn't portend good fortunes, you think pessimistically. Still, you have no choice but to carry on, so you pass the glass corridor on your right and soon arrive at another set of doors. The sign welcomes you to the Geranium Unit with a picture of a five-petalled purple flower. This doesn't tell you what to expect inside, but you decide to enter anyway. Turn to **258**.

You approach the double doors of the ward and see the flowery sign above: 'Welcome to Forget-me-not Ward'. That seems a strange choice for the geriatric ward but still, it looks clean and well cared for in its Victorian style. You pass by a few offices and storerooms but are soon in the main body of the ward. There is a large desk in the middle of the room, separating the opposing rows of beds. Everything is in place and even the sheets have hospital corners. For a second, you're tempted to curl up and sleep on one of the beds or you could just plough on and explore the far end of the ward. You can see signs for the bathroom and the patients' day room. Where will you go?

To the bed for a sleep   Turn to **329**

To the bathroom   Turn to **217**

To the day room   Turn to **112**

You crouch down next to Daniel's chair, watching the precarious strand of saliva waiver with each rattling breath.

'Hello sir,' you ask, thinking that politeness might just help, 'Can you tell me anything?' The old man raises his head and looks straight at you, while he sucks the spittle back up over his lips. It's disgusting to watch, but you try not to show it.

'Oh yes. Do you know...' the pause stretches on and on until finally, he continues. 'The colour yellow is good for mental stimulation.' And with that, he slumps back down again, all mental stimulation apparently exhausted.

You stand up and leave the day room (turn to **315**).

If this is your first time in this stairwell, you're going to be shocked to see a curled up human skeleton nestled half-way up the stairs. If you'd already met the skeleton, you pass by it without batting an eyelid. At this stage, you're getting quite blasé and are wondering if anything can shock you ever again. The answer to that comes quickly, as you take the final corner and almost trip over the black, wispy cocoon, which is writhing on the landing. You leap back, falling down a couple of stairs before you catch your balance, then watch in horror as it draws itself up. Is it about to explode?

'Beware the Witchfinder General,' a booming voice announces, the words echoing up and down the stairwell. 'His work here continues!' With that, the cocoon slumps down, then scoots off up the wall and through an almost invisible vent in the ceiling. The only thing left of the encounter is a few black streaks. Once you've calmed down and your heart is beating normally again, you leave the stairwell. The first-floor corridor looks the same as it did the last time you were here, only now you're not just wandering around aimlessly. You need to get out of here and if you've already found a clue of who can help you to do just that, you should also be able to pinpoint a destination. So where do you go?

Back into the operating theatres   Turn to **366**
Prayer room   Turn to **151**
Vascular ward   Turn to **212**

358

You get a glass of water from the small kitchen and bring it to her lips. With no jawbone, she struggles to drink, so you pour a little into her parched mouth. After a little cough, she smiles gratefully and remarks that it has been a long time since she felt any kindness.

'Who did this to you?' you ask.

'Dr Robert Carmichael. You must have heard of him. His notoriety surely stretches far from this world.' You shake your head and wait for her to continue.

'He's a monster to his core and has been for an eternity. He's looking for body parts. They're special, they're important to him. He's killed many, many women to get his hands on them.' Her voice fades away; she sounds tired.

'But what do you mean? He takes trophies? He's a serial killer? Is that who killed my friend?'

But she shakes her head as if your very presence is exhausting her. Just when you think she's fallen asleep, she raises her eyelids and stares directly at you.

'Please stop him. I need to die now. It's been too long.'

She sinks into herself and although you ask, 'How? How can I stop him?' there's no response. Although you've learnt something here, there are still many more questions than answers. You leave this ward where bones used to be mended, not excised then cast aside.

Turn to **30**.

359

The door swings open easily, and the room is identical to the others, except it doesn't appear to be so unused. There is an old leather suitcase under the bed and a worn notebook on the desk. You open the pages of the book and see precise, small handwriting in black ink detailing the preparation and administration of soap enemas. Lovely! Definitely a nurses' residence, you think, although there is a small door in the left-hand corner of the room. That's unusual…

You can now either have a rummage through the desk drawers (turn to **144**), look inside the suitcase (turn to **383**) or head directly to the small door (turn to **66**).

He may think that he's all powerful and demonic, but you believe that he's still a man who's under the control of a demon. That means, his name is what his name has always been. You start to scratch out 'Carmichael', wincing as the knife scrapes over the blackboard, but then you hear a more piercing sound. Out of the corner of your eye, you can see Carmichael writhing in agony. He seems to be collapsing in on himself as all his life-force is drained. When the name is completely obliterated, you turn to the withered figure on the floor. He's still alive but only just. You can hear the death rattle in his throat. What will you do now?

Exit the lecture theatre immediately	Turn to **394**
Take the knife and behead him	Turn to **72**
Lean over him until he's dead	Turn to **133**

361

The one-eyed woman seems to be in charge — maybe that's the advantage of having an eye — and says,

'The two doors lead to death or safety. A sister can answer one question from you, but you should know that one sister will only lie and the other will only tell the truth. Which one is which? I don't know. Now ask your question'.

You think quickly then say to one of the blind old women: 'If I ask your other sister, which door leads to safety, what would she say?' The hag brushes the straggly tendrils from her face, then points to the door that is directly facing you. Well, that's her answer but which door *will* you take?

The door directly facing you   Turn to **78**
The right-hand side door   Turn to **265**

362

The door sweeps shut behind you and you feel an inkling of relief that the vermin can't take you by surprise by flooding out. It's perhaps the only silver lining with this black cloud…

Now though, you need to decide whether to continue along the passageway by going right (turn to **299**) or left (turn to **159**) Alternatively, you could investigate the orthopaedic ward opposite if you haven't done so already (turn to **65**).

She is beautiful and petite and when she gently says, 'You must be confused', you can hear a distinct French accent. Strangely, she is also holding a stuffed toy. There are many for sale for the children in paediatrics and she happens to be cradling a plush fox, stroking its bushy tail. Eventually, you agree that you are confused. Her smile softens, and she nods sympathetically.

'When I was a child, I loved to look out of my window and see the Eiffel Tower growing as it was built. If you find a room that has a link to my home city, you can trigger the secret passageway that will help you to leave this place. You must draw a circle, step in it and say these words: Teeth and bones and brick-red flame; Stand within the circle frame; Line the passageway with string; Give your thanks to Baigujing.'

With prompting, you repeat the words, stumbling over the name Baigujing. She pronounces each syllable slowly: By-goo-shing, making sure that you can say it.

'You should go now,' she finally states.

'But who are you? Are you trapped here too? How *old* are you?' you ask in a rapid-fire delivery. This time, she smiles and gently shakes her head, then turns, crouches down and starts talking to the fox. It seems that the conversation with you is over.

If you think you've found the location that has a connection with the city that the Eiffel Tower is in and want to trigger the secret passageway, **subtract 100** from that section and turn to the new one.

The angry man has gone into a storeroom, although he made a strange clanking sound as he went, so there's nothing else in the shop for you. You decide to leave and continue along the thoroughfare. Turn to **260**.

364

'That's *not* the right answer!' they say disdainfully and in unison, then resume their vigil over the coloured bricks, and although you try to cajole some conversation from them, it's clear that they are done with you. You have no option but to leave the room. Turn to **398**.

365

You walk past a door on your left and are surprised to hear the soft voices of children coming from within. If you want to see if you can talk to these children, turn to **182**. On the other hand, if you think they sound far too creepy, carry on straight ahead (turn to **120**).

366

You push open the door to the operating theatres and enter, but before you can take another step, a hand grabs you by the throat and slams you off your feet, back against the door. You feel something crack in your spine — a momentous pain followed by a weird nothingness. Your legs dangle uselessly, as the man grabs you underneath the armpits and hoists you over his shoulder. You can smell the blood soaked into his clothing. Nancy's blood.

'Did you really think that you could get away from me by guessing? Nobody guesses here. You either know or you die. My Master is going to be very happy to get the twelfth one. The *last* one! Very happy indeed.' He carries you off and as your head bangs repeatedly against his back with every step, you wonder: Which body part is going to be harvested?

367

You unravel the paper and see just 3 sentences on it — it appears to be the clues for the combination lock.

The first is the number of bones in the ear

The second the number of chambers in the heart

The third is the number of babies being carried, if a woman has quintuplets.

If you know the answers to these clues, you should dial in the correct code and turn to the section with this 3-digit number. If you don't know the answer, you can't unlock the door, so you'll just have to head back to the junction (turn to **210**).

368

You carry on along the corridor and see the remnants of iron bed frames in cold, depressing rooms until finally, you come to a junction. One passageway continues straight on (turn to **122**) and the other takes a sharp right (turn to **236**), but both look dark and miserable. Where do you want to head now?

369

You bring your face down to the vessel, close your eyes, open your mouth and hope for the best. With a low, drawn-out moan, Carmichael's dying breath sidles out and, in a heavy mist, settles over the other ingredients. For a second, nothing happens, but then a spark and a hot, dense flame erupt. You concentrate with all your might, willing the right coloured smoke to curl up from the blaze. Which colour do you want it to be?

White	Turn to **124**
Black	Turn to **232**

370

Just ahead is the entrance to the Recovery bay and a little further on is the staircase, which leads downstairs to more operating theatres. You want to get out of this oppressive darkness, so if you decide to try your luck downstairs, turn to **388**. If you'd prefer to head to the Recovery area, turn to **117**.

371

You grasp the blue snake amulet and thrust it towards Jezebeth's face. You are rewarded by a flicker of shock in those black eyes, so you throw it to the floor and stamp on it. The demon gives a shriek, a cry of fury and anguish, so you keep on trampling the gemstones. Breathing heavily, you eventually stop and are stunned to see that Jezebeth is still stood there. Turn to **14**.

372

It takes a little while to rip away the glued-on pages, but eventually you force open the door and step into a scene from a charnel house. There are streaks of blood over the walls and puddles collecting on the floor. It looks like something's tried to clean up but only succeeded in spreading the copious crimson fluid around the room. There is a soft thrum of insects, but you can't see where they are. At one side of the room, the curtains are pulled around what you presume is a bed. At the opposite side is a door wedged half-open with a discarded mop. You can either find out what's behind the curtains (turn to **252**) or go to the door (turn to **53**).

373

You shuffle forward, slow and steady, but then you hear something. At first, you think it's a draught and hope this means you're close to an exit, but soon the sound becomes more discernible. A slight fluttering of wings and occasional scratching of talons. You gulp and peer up pointlessly in the darkness, wondering, 'What is up there?' If you have a candle, you could light it, but maybe the flame would disturb and awaken whatever it is. Momentarily stumped, you weigh up the pros and cons. What should you do?

Light the candle   Turn to **88**
Creep along in the dark   Turn to **317**

374

You walk down this narrow corridor, recognising that the grime and decay from before has gone. Here, everything looks clean, albeit old-fashioned. You look up and notice that there are no lights in the ceiling either, but there's no time to dwell on that. You reach the door and cautiously turn the handle. Immediately, you are assailed by a strong gust from within and a strange, otherworldly, flapping sound…

If you want to enter the room, turn to **178**, but if not, you should go back to the junction where you can choose to go straight on (turn to **134**) or take a right and go towards the staircase (turn to **206**).

After only one step, you feel a distinct burning against your thigh. You halt and pull the bag away from your body. A small patch of the cotton is already blackened and smoking and your scrubs has a singed mark on it.

'Bloody Hell!' you mutter, as you rummage around in the bag, looking for the culprit. At the bottom, you find it. A smouldering and half-melted petri dish, the once pink sea eagle talons now a charcoal powder. You hurl it away and but you don't hear it hit the floor. That's strange! You get your torch out and aim it forward, then gasp and stagger back.

There is a huge, deep pit in front of you. Another step and you'd have fallen right in it! Once the nauseating sense of vertigo has eased, you go back into the Children's Ward and head for the junction. Turn to **9**.

You grab a nearby lead for the EEG machine and start wiggling it around on the floor. The cat watches, instantly alert. It's working, you think, as the cat goes into a stalking position, tail flicking from side to side. You move gradually to the other side of the room, bringing the cat away from the bed, but then you hear,

'Are you going to play with that all day? Or are you actually going to attach the lead, so we can get some recordings done? Don't get me wrong. I'm grateful to have an assistant, but you will have to do some work, you know!' The cat, now sat on its haunches, stares at you with an undisguised look of disdain. You stand there, EEG lead hanging limply in your hand and totally lost for words.

'Dumb in all meanings of the word!' the cat proclaims before leaping back up onto the bed to adjust the position of an electrode. It pauses briefly to look back and shout 'Get out!' which you do. Turn to **126**.

377

Thankfully, you pass the bodies without incidence but there's something about this space — it just doesn't *feel* right. You speed up, breaking into a half-jog when... Bam! You slam into... Thin air? You nearly knocked yourself out and now you're dazed, but when you stretch out an arm, your fingers touch something solid but invisible. You trace the form and the realisation hits you. It's a glass cube and you're in the middle of it. You're trapped. Hysterically, you start kicking and bashing your fists against it which is why you don't notice the hissing sound. Your last thought is 'Everything's spinning' as the carbon monoxide reaches a critical level. You slump down, dead before you even hit the floor. The cube disappears as inexplicably as it arrived and small, strange creatures laugh as they drag your corpse over to the nearest available bench.

You leap forward, knife raised, ready to swipe through his windpipe, when… He disappears. You drop the knife in shock and it clatters onto the floorboards. In the following silence, you hear a small laugh behind you. He's now stood on the highest tier of the gallery, looking down at you. Of course, teleportation. But why didn't he use a power directly on you? Your eyes rest on the fallen knife — it was protecting you! In the same instant that you try to pick it back up, you feel a strange sensation wash over your body. It's like someone else is controlling your body and you can only watch helplessly as you reach over the operating table, pick the cleaver up and slam it down against your wrist. The bone shatters and blood spurts from the stump. As the room starts to spin, you know that you've made the gravest of errors but it's too late now to get it right.

379

You place the golden goblet on the table and take a deep breath. This is really happening. If you can do this right, you just might make it back. You feel a little trickle of sweat weave down your temple, then you pull the photo out of the bag. You have no idea how the image of you ended up in the mortuary, but it must mean something. You are the executioner, after all, so with a decisive move, you crumple up the photo and stuff it into the goblet. Next, you're going to mix it with some blood. If you have a recipe of this spell, you should know where to take the blood from; if not, you'll just have to guess and keep your fingers crossed. Which organ do you squeeze until the blood drips into the goblet?

The heart (turn to **82**) or the uterus (turn to **320**).

380

At the last second, you look at the narrow gap between door and frame and see the faint bloodied footprint on the floor. It's him! The murderer must be in there! Holding your breath and desperately trying not to make a sound, you set off down the corridor towards stairwell A (turn to **323**).

381

Trying to quash the rising sense of panic, you desperately think of how to summon Jezebeth. You call out her name. Nothing. You start pulling out drawers. Nothing. You empty your bag onto the floor, and just when you are rifling through the contents, searching for a clue, you hear the pharmacy door open. You look up, breathing rapidly and very, very scared. It is the assassin. Still dressed in black. Still carrying a knife and still obviously planning to kill you. He takes a step towards you.

If you earlier accidently inhaled furnace ash, turn to **87**.
If you avoided breathing in the cremains, turn to **198**.

It's a relief to be in this wide and airy passageway. The skylights in the vaulted roof let the bright sunshine warm your bones after the gloom of the asylum ward. In a short while, you reach a door. The small sign states that you've arrived at the Sleep Disorders Laboratory, but the flamboyant and flowery declaration above the door is 'Welcome to Poppy Ward'. Poppy? Someone's quirky sense of humour, you suppose. You push open the door (turn to **223**).

383

You yank the suitcase out from under the bed, press the two clasps to unlock it and are rewarded with a smell of moth balls and faded woollens. It's not a resounding success, you think but persevere, rummaging through to see if there's anything else in there.

Ow! You whip your hand back, but a drop of blood is already forming on your palm. What was that? After some cautious probing, you find the culprit: a glass syringe with a steel needle, and filled with…? You pick up a brown bottle labelled 'laudanum'. Oh great! You start to feel a little bit dizzy as the opiate circulates, but it wasn't a large enough amount to cause serious problems. You abandon your search and instead head for the small door. Turn to **66**.

384

You grasp the blue snake amulet and thrust it towards Jezebeth's face. You are rewarded by a flicker of shock in those black eyes and before you give yourself a chance to change your mind, you throw it to the floor and stamp on it. The demon gives a shriek, a cry of fury and anguish, so you keep on trampling the gemstones. Breathing heavily, you eventually stop and are stunned to see that Jezebeth is still stood there. Turn to **14**.

385

You crouch down next to Daniel's chair, watching the precarious strand of saliva waiver with each rattling breath.

'Hello sir,' you ask, thinking that politeness might just help, 'Can you tell me anything?' The old man raises his head and looks straight at you, while he sucks the spittle back up over his lips. It's disgusting to watch but you try not to show it.

'Oh yes. Do you know…' the pause stretches on and on, until finally he continues. 'The colour yellow is good for mental stimulation.' And with that, he slumps back down again, all mental stimulation apparently exhausted.

You stand up and leave the day room (turn to **201**).

You stand in front of the mirror, momentarily shocked at how haggard you look. There are purple shadows underneath your eyes and your pallor has a distinctly waxy hue. As you peer at yourself, you think that your vision is going blurry too but stepping back, you can see that the mirror itself is misting over. Once the surface is totally obliterated, words start appearing, as though an invisible finger is doodling in the condensation. It's a riddle.

**My first is in WITCH but not in CHASTE
My second is in SIN but not in WASTE
My third is in LOVE but not in VEX
My fourth is in HOLE but not in HEX
My fifth is in MOON but not in MAIN
My last is in WICCA but not in VAIN
My whole has a sap that will soothe when you're ill
And whose name is the same as when tears start to spill**

If you know what the answer is, turn the word into a number by using the code: A=1, B=2, C=3 ….. Z=26. Add the numbers together and turn to the section with the same number.

If you don't know the answer, the mist gradually clears, taking the riddle with it and you can either choose to look at the statue (turn to **244**) or go through the double doors (turn to **41**).

387

Back in the small, dingy foyer, you look around and weigh up your options. Where do you go now?

Storeroom	Turn to **164**
Furnace	Turn to **219**
Mortuary	Turn to **6**

388

You push open the door and step into the narrow, windowless stairwell. It was used only by Theatre staff, diving up and down, fetching random equipment or new stock. You smile briefly at the memory — it was one way to keep fit! On the third step, the emergency lighting cuts out and the darkness is total and impenetrable. You clutch the bannister until your heart calms down. After all, you've often joked that you could find your way around here blindfolded. Once the pulse has cleared from your ears, you listen. Nothing. Everything's OK. Isn't it? Once you've prised your hand off the bannister, you could continue down the stairs (turn to **71**) but if this has shaken you up too much, you should exit the stairwell (turn to **207**).

You step out of the blackness and into a thin, cold, concrete corridor. The fluorescent bulbs are flickering but you can see that it stretches on until a sharp right turn at the end. You jog along at a fair pace, occasionally turning to check that nothing is following you from the cavern but other than the electric hum of the lights, all is quiet. You take the corner and directly ahead of you is a door. As you walk towards it, you sense a slight give in the floor and jump to the side, fearing that the ground is about to collapse underneath you. However, when you look closer, you can see that it's actually a trapdoor. Where do you want to go now? If you want to take the door ahead, turn to **167**, but if you'd rather go through the trapdoor, turn to **324**.

390

Being on the floor, you are disadvantaged, and he knows it. He smirks, then bolts forward. You try to leap away, but stumble. You fall inches away from him and know that you can't escape. He raises the blade, but then you cough. It comes from nowhere, with no warning, but you cough and a cloud of grey ash is ejected from your mouth. As it erupts out, you remember the ash you breathed in from the furnace — it's come back! It engulfs him and instantly, he starts clawing at his throat. The cremains pour into his mouth, choking and suffocating him, as the burnt witches finally take their revenge. After a few minutes, he lies dead in front of you, a ghastly grimace fixed on his face, but before you can get to grips with what's just happened, you sense another presence in the room. Jezebeth has arrived. Turn to **149**.

391

You push open the doors and leave the x-ray department. Marching resolutely along, you soon pass the glass corridor on your right and arrive at another set of doors. The sign welcomes you to the Geranium Unit with a simple picture of a five-petalled purple flower. This doesn't tell you what to expect inside, but you decide to enter anyway (turn to **258**).

392

You are midway down the passageway when something gets your full attention! There is a black wispy mass attached to the wall. It's only the size of a watermelon but it looks suspiciously like a cocoon and you're sure you can see it writhing. You have a vision of it exploding with a scurry of thousands of spiders, so you give it a wide berth, while you consider your next move. To the right is the general surgery ward. You can hear a faint yet frenetic squeaking from inside, but if you still want to enter, turn to **45**. Opposite that is the orthopaedic ward (turn to **65**) or you could just continue along the corridor (turn to **299**).

Empusa gives an excited clap of her hands, then tucks her leg underneath her and leans forward.

'Well, it's all because of Carmichael's mother,' she begins, and you nod encouragingly. 'She was a cruel and controlling woman. She put him down, humiliated him and abused him. It was no surprise that he grew up hating all women and wanted them to suffer. He thought that when he became a doctor that would be enough to earn him respect but no. He always felt that the nurses and midwives were correcting him or telling him that he'd done things wrong, even though he had done things wrong. He started killing them as a way of relieving these frustrations, but when his wife couldn't get pregnant, he believed that he was being mocked and that they were gloating about their own fertility. This was when he started excising organs to fathom the mysteries of womanhood, as he saw it.' Empusa paused, shaking her head and then she gathered herself and carried on.

'Jezebeth had been watching the entire time. She's drawn to this kind of madness and she waited. She didn't have to wait long. Carmichael was in the midst of a frenzied slaughter. He had totally lost control and was in a rage. He thought that it made him powerful and fearful but to the contrary. He *lost* control, so Jezebeth was able to *take* control. There and then, she took him over and he'd been unwittingly under her command ever since.' Empusa sits back, staring at her hands, draped loosely in her lap. 'It's a sad story, but maybe you can give it a happy ending.' She looks so hopeful that you feel obliged to nod and say that you'll try your best. Empusa gives a faint smile but sits slumped on her stool. It seems like your audience is over. You can now either leave straight away (turn to **255**), or you could have a nosy around first and examine the fridge (turn to **303**).

394

Halfway up these steep, narrow stairs, you catch sight of something underneath the wooden pews. As much as you'd like to leave the shrivelled corpse of Carmichael behind, your nosiness gets the better of you. You crouch down and grope beneath the seat before grabbing hold of a heavy box. There is something inside it, but the box is locked. Do you have a small brass key? If so, turn to the section with the same number that was engraved on the key. If you don't have one, there is no way you can prise the box open, so you shove it bad-temperedly away and leave the lecture theatre. Turn to **147**.

395

Jezebeth looks you up and down, but what is she searching for? Eventually, she gives a whip-crack flick of the tail and glares furiously at you. Suddenly, you realise. Of course! She was trying to take control of you but couldn't, and now you feel emboldened. It's time to strike back! Turn to **3**.

396

You step forward and crouch down in front of the girl, although you're really not sure what you're going to say next — you're just going to have to wing it!

'Don't worry,' you say. 'I'll take care of you,' and you reach out to take her hand. Funnily enough, her eyes seem to be beady and black and if you really concentrate, you can see her tongue flicking in and out... Come to think of it, that doesn't feel like a hand either. It's scaly and muscular and... In a split-second, it has wrapped around your arm, an immensely strong spiral that you cannot pull off. It coils around your shoulder then chest and as you feel it squeeze, you know that you haven't a chance. You let out a breath and it constricts further — only a little but it's enough. You can't take a breath in now and your final sight is of the snake unhinging its jaw. You're going to make a tasty feast for this reptile.

397

The wrought iron spiral staircase is narrow with deep steps and you grip tightly onto the bannister as you descend. Round and round, deeper and deeper — how far does this staircase go? Your footsteps make a loud clanging noise which echoes around, but then you realise that it's not just echoes. There's someone following you!

You whip around, almost slipping and falling. The figure, just four steps behind you, is dressed in a lab coat but has blue-grey skin. He looks unkempt as if he's not slept in days. For a few seconds, you just stare at each other. He doesn't move any closer but gestures futilely, as if he hasn't a clue what to say. Eventually, he waves his hand at his own face and says, 'Argyria' in a broad Yorkshire accent.

'What?' you reply, thinking, *is that his name?*

'Argyria,' he repeats, 'He makes us experiment with silver solutions. Makes us drink them. It turns the skin this colour. Silver's the answer, he keeps saying.'

'He?' you ask and then a thought occurs to you. If you think you know who he's talking about, you could say the name and that might prompt this lab technician to tell you more. But which name do you say?

Sir Joseph Lister	Turn to **76**
Dr Robert Carmichael	Turn to **330**
Mr Rasmus Jansson	Turn to **110**

398

You are back in the pink corridor and must decide where to go now. You could continue straight on until you reach the last room on the left if you haven't done so already (turn to **273**) or go to the junction and take the corridor out of the ward (turn to **50**).

Although, this large room is free of flora, the emerald green makes you feel like you've walked into a lush forest. Around the edge of the room are the incubators, but the monitors and machines are silent. You creep forward and recoil as you see the tiny form lying inside the nearest cot. You don't think there's anything you can do for the baby, but it feels wrong to leave it like this. You step even closer and realise with a mixture of relief and anger that it's not actually a baby; it's just a doll. Who would do that? As your heart rate returns to normal, you survey the room. Other than the incubators, there is nothing much here but there is another door to your left. If you'd like to simply leave the room, you could go back into the ivy-covered corridor (turn to **7**) or head over to the other door (turn to **211**), but if you're curious to see if all the incubators contain dolls, turn to **128**.

For the longest time, you stand there staring at the floor, at the spot where Jezebeth disappeared. You are unable to move or even think. Is it really over? You collapse to the ground overwhelmed by dizziness, but grateful for the unconsciousness that cocoons you.

You wake up with a start. The darkness confuses you at first. Where are you? With your heart thudding in your chest, you grope aimlessly around, trying to get your bearings. You're lying across functional and slightly sticky faux-leather chairs. Oh, that's right. You give a relieved sigh as your eyes adjust to the gloominess and you can now make out the furniture in the small break room. How long had you been… Hang on a minute! Haven't you done all this before? What's going on?

You grope your way in the dark and open the door. A dull, flickering light illuminates the familiar corridor and you walk cautiously to the other break room. You can't hear anything, no drip-drip-drip this time, but you never know. You peer tentatively into the room and a scream pierces the silence. You freeze and then you hear… laughter? You look towards the sound and see Nancy clutching her chest but laughing hysterically. In between breaths, she manages to say, 'I must've nodded off. You scared me to death.'

She's alive!. Was it all a dream? All that happened with Carmichael and Jezebeth – was that just a delusional nightmare? Nancy carries on chattering; she doesn't seem to have noticed how weird you're acting.

'Mind you,' she continues, 'I'm not feeling too great. My throat's really sore; it's like I've swallowed something sharp or maybe I'm getting the flu.'

Then she looks up. 'What on Earth happened to you?'

You don't know what she means, so look quizzically back at her and Nancy points at your scrubs. You look down and see that you're covered in a fine black soot. For a second, you stare in disbelief, then rush to the bathroom. You hear Nancy asking if you're OK, but you can only stare in the mirror. The black spiral branding is still there on your back, although it's no longer fresh and tender — it looks like it's been there for years.

You're not sure how long you stay there, trying to work it all out, but, in the end, all you can do is shrug your shoulders and accept that it really happened.

So you wipe yourself down with your, thankfully, intact hands and smile tearfully to yourself — you made it through the nightshift!

Meanwhile, somewhere else, far away…Turn to **401**.

The black wispy mass writhes, its undulations becoming increasingly frenetic, until finally, the cocoon starts to morph into a more recognisable form. A cluster of figures face it — they look furious and one says,

'What happened to leaving the experiment to run its course? No interference, you said! Just observations, you said!'

'Altering variables can be a valid option given the right circumstances.' It responds defensively and somewhat, weakly. 'I just wanted to give this one a chance. Jezebeth was being… Well, you know.'

There is a snort from the Cluster, then one of them bangs their fist down on the table and states vehemently:

'It's my turn now!'

Valuable Information and Collected Items

48172120R00150